Big Foot Stole My Wife!

Other Five Star Titles
by Joan Hess:

Death of a Romance Writer and Other Stories
Malice in Maggody
Martians in Maggody

Big Foot Stole My Wife! and Other Stories

JOAN HESS

Five Star • Waterville, Maine

This collection of stories is a work of fiction. Names, characters, places and incidents are either the product of the author's imagination, or, if real, used fictitiously.

First Edition
First Printing: February 2003

Published in 2003 in conjunction with Tekno Books and
Ed Gorman.

Set in 11 pt. Plantin by Christina S. Huff.

Printed in the United States on permanent paper.

Library of Congress Cataloging-in-Publication Data

Hess, Joan.
    Big Foot stole my wife! : and other stories / by Joan Hess.
       p. cm.—(Five Star first edition mystery series)
    Contents: Big Foot stole my wife!—Paper trail—Heptagon—
    Make yourself at home—All that glitters—The cremains of the
    day—Dead on arrival—The last to know—The Maggody files,
    D.W.I.—The Maggody files, death in Bloom—Another room.
    ISBN 0-7862-4318-X (hc : alk. paper)
    1. Detective and mystery stories, American.   I. Title.
    II. Series.
PS3558.E79785 B5 2003
    813'.54—dc21   2002043053

Big Foot Stole My Wife!
and Other Stories

Contents

Big Foot Stole My Wife!   9

Paper Trail   33

Heptagon   59

Make Yourselves at Home   70

All That Glitters   90

The Cremains of the Day   113

Dead on Arrival   129

The Last to Know   144

The Maggody Files: D.W.I.   166

The Maggody Files: Death in Bloom   183

Another Room   195

Big Foot Stole My Wife!

Jay Jay Anderson read the tabloid headline, not once but over and over and over again, as if each subsequent time might produce an entirely new declaration. It did not. He tightened his grip on the bottle of Perrier, the plastic bag holding three limes, a similar container of arugula, and the crinkly package of rice crackers. "Big Foot Stole My Wife."

"Sure, he did," Jay Jay murmured. "That's what I'd say, too."

A stout woman with blue hair and a bunch of bananas stared over her shoulder at him. "I beg your pardon?"

"Inquiring minds want to know," Jay Jay said, pointing with his grocery list at the tabloid in the metal rack. "Those things pander to the morbid side of human nature, don't you think?"

Apparently comforted by his impeccably conservative clothes, trimmed hair, and boyish face, she gave him a vague nod and turned back to glower at the inconsiderate soul with nine items in the express lane—which was clearly labeled eight items, cash only. Jay Jay also glowered, being the sort who would never defy the laws that governed the express lane at Consumers Market. If one's list had nine items, one planned accordingly for the necessity of a slight delay in the standard lanes. The express lane was for the use of those with foresight. The inconsiderate soul was now further delaying Blue Hair and Jay Jay by the writing of a check. Perhaps the Big Foot of the produce department would come lumbering down the aisle, slobbering and slathering and searching for Those Who Deserved to Die.

Corkie deserved to die. Jay Jay arched his eyebrows and mentally listed eight reasons why she deserved to die, then halted out of deference to the express lane sign. The eight were in the spirit of the seven deadly sins, with indiscriminate promiscuity thrown in to make a tidy octet.

Blue Hair huffed away and Jay Jay lay down his items, produced cash, counted his change, and carried the sack to his tawny BMW. As he pulled into traffic, he tried to recall his emotions when he'd first met his wife, Charlotte "Corkie" McNevins Anderson. She'd been as sleek as his car, as golden, as eager to purr when he pushed down on the accelerator, as redolent of the softest and most expensive leather. Quality, he'd decided by the second date, and exactly what he needed. He promptly (and successfully) had devised a plan to win both her heart and access to the family fortune.

Now, ten years later, her purr was shrill. The sleek lines were harsh angles; the redolence was a miasma of ashtrays and booze (her nickname having arisen in prep school from an infamous predilection for that beverage constrained by corks). Her erstwhile golden hair changed colors weekly, as a result of lengthy sessions in the salon, and as he carefully changed lanes in anticipation of a turn, Jay Jay found himself wondering if he would recognize her should she step into the street. There was no doubt in his mind that if he did, he would run her down with only a second's hesitation to devise a convincing defense.

But if it were not convincing, life would become intolerable. The scenario included policemen, lawyers, juries, and a judge; the bottom line was an unpleasant future in cohabitation with the criminal element of the lower class. A pervert for a roommate. Crude clothing. A diet consisting only of cheap, starchy carbohydrates. Limited exercise inside a fenced square. Neckless, uneducated brutes with the power to bully him. No corner office, no stunningly beautiful and compliant secretary, no racquetball at lunch, no eighteen holes on the weekend, no carefully choreographed networking in the locker room, no wondrous car. An institutional lifestyle was not in his plan.

Jay Jay drove at a moderate rate down the tree-lined streets, noting the plethora of European cars, the mansions, the manicured yards, the designer-dressed children frolicking like thoroughbred colts, which of course they were. He did not want to lose this utopia, this enclave of wealth and power and gentility. He couldn't kill Corkie.

And he couldn't divorce her, either, although it was painfully clear that his acquisition had been a grievous error, attributable to youthful zeal and miscalculation. Corkie was hardly more than a marginal asset, and her value depreciated annually. He had first realized the enormity of his mistake when their portfolio had reached an appropriate level to begin a family. He had presented her with the glad tidings and suggested they commence the procreation of a respectable number of offspring to please her father and ensure the continuity of the family fortune. She had scoffed. Over the years he had requested on numerous occasions that she serve as hostess to those who would aid the dazzling escalation of his career. She had sneered. Her disdainful attempts too often had ended in drunken disaster. Yes, she had continually scoffed and sneered and stumbled, forcing him to make detours along his carefully plotted journey through life. Jay Jay detested detours. He detested his wife.

It wasn't as though she would object to a divorce, in that she had told him on many occasions how thoroughly she detested him. But a divorce would destroy the years spent on each rung of the ladder—the series of goals thus far achieved, the goals that glittered within his reach in the future. Corkie's father, also known as the chairman of the board of the conservative investment firm that supplied the corner office, the secretary, the racquetball court, the membership in the country club, and the car, would harrumph and then fire his ex–son-in-law more briskly than he could say high-yield zero coupon treasury bill.

Noting a stoplight at the end of the next block, Jay Jay instinctively braked so that the light would change to green seconds before he reached the intersection. No, if he was to have a million invested in blue chips and municipal bonds by fifty, a townhouse in New York by fifty-five, a condo in Palm Springs by sixty, followed by a golden retirement of golf, travel, exquisite art, aged brandy, prudent philanthropy, and all the other items noted in a leather-bound journal, he couldn't divorce Corkie. Beginning anew at thirty-six would play havoc with the game plan.

"I wonder if Big Foot hires out," he said as he parked behind Corkie's Cadillac—big, flashy, ostentatious, marred by dents and scratches (and therefore due to be replaced before too long). It was unfortunate that wives could not be replaced in an equally efficient manner. He went through the kitchen door and left the sack on the counter. Next to the sink the gin bottle was half empty, the vermouth scarcely touched. An ashtray piled high with red-stained cigarette butts smoldered, sending up a tendril of acrid smoke.

As he curled his lip, he had a whimsical thought, and despite his innate aversion to such things, he paused to analyze it. Thus did Jay Jay Anderson, while standing in the middle of his kitchen, a pensive frown tugging at his mouth and two creases marring his brow (but not his trousers), conceive of an outrageously bold—yet potentially workable—plan to murder his wife.

The preliminary groundwork took several months, but Jay Jay permitted neither impatience nor impetuosity to discolor his methodology, aware that a single lapse might result in a fatal error (and a lengthy sentence, since premeditation was indicated). While Corkie obliviously spent the summer at the club, he haunted public libraries to ascertain where best to orchestrate his plan. He peered at an endless stream of microfiche newspapers, all the while making notes that were kept in an unmarked manila folder. He consulted atlases, anthropological studies, topographies, and past issues of *The Farmer's Almanac.* Once he had selected date and location, he wrote his dialogue, which had to sound spontaneous despite heavy editing, and then rehearsed both in his car and, when conditions permitted, in front of the mirror in the executive washroom. One night he stayed at the office and taped his lines, then dissected each in terms of enunciation and inflection. The results of his labor were more than satisfactory.

Over the course of the summer, each contingency was addressed. Eventually, through diligence, each contingency was covered.

"I've rented a cabin for a month," he announced one evening when he felt his wife was sufficiently sloshed and therefore disinclined to violence.

"A cabin? How utterly absurd." Corkie swirled the gin in her glass, ogling the tumbling olive with a predatory glint.

"The very word gives me hives. What ever could have come over you?"

"Oh it's not really a cabin," Jay Jay said, chuckling. "I've done research on it. It's a summer lodge in Vermont, built by a very rich old family as a retreat, and quite luxurious. All the modern conveniences, terribly elegant, good antiques, fireplaces in all the bedrooms, sauna and hot tub, screened-in porches to keep out the pests, that sort of thing. You'll love it, honey."

She sucked in the olive and rolled it around her mouth. Jay Jay watched with idle optimism, hoping that she might inadvertently inhale it and choke to death. To his regret, she gulped it down and said, "Now why would I love it? I cannot imagine a month in Vermont, much less a month with only you for company. You're so proper and predictable that I'd expire from boredom after thirty minutes. My shrink says you're a classic example of anal-retentive. In any case, I'd rather spend a month in hell than in this remote place for even an hour."

Taking her glass, Jay Jay crossed to the wet bar and fixed a martini for her and a glass of Perrier for himself. She had a point. It was difficult to envision her gathering autumn leaves for a centerpiece on a pine table, or frying fish in a cast iron skillet. But he had anticipated the inevitability of her initial resistance, and was looking forward to the next series of countermoves with some degree of amusement.

He sat down beside her and offered a mild argument to gauge the depth of her resistance. "You've been so busy playing golf and tennis this summer that I thought you might enjoy a chance to get away for a few weeks and simply lounge around all day. You wouldn't have to fuss with your hair or clothes, or even bother to put on makeup."

"And look like something the cat wouldn't bother to drag

in? What a divine suggestion." She lit a cigarette and blew a cloud of smoke into his face. "Besides, I happen to enjoy my afternoons at the club. This house is so dreary, especially when you're here, and there are so many interesting people at the club with whom to drink and chatter. This cabin of yours would be a veritable mausoleum."

"But it would be so tranquil, my dearest, and relaxing. Besides, I think it might be expedient to avoid the club for a few weeks, don't you?"

"Not particularly," Corkie said with a yawn. She sent a cloud into his face, then ground out the cigarette and lit another.

Jay Jay shook his head in gentle admonishment. "Perhaps you might reconsider, my dear. You know that I make every effort not to meddle with your . . . ah, friendships. However, this . . . ah, friendship with the greenskeeper at the club is beginning to raise a few eyebrows among our set. Borwaski is hardly in your class. He's crude, unintelligible, and illiterate. His beetlish brow and beady little eyes are symptomatic of generations of inbreeding. He reeks of fertilizer and sweat. To be frank, he resembles a very unpleasant gorilla, and I should hate for anyone to assume that you and he have been and continue to be, ah, intimate friends. It might prove the death of you—socially, that is."

"He is a brute, isn't he? I can't imagine why the board members keep him on." Corkie gave her husband a beatific smile, but her hand was trembling as she held out her glass for a refill. "But no one has any reason to think I'd allow him to paw me in some sleazy motel."

"But people eventually do notice that sort of liaison, no matter how carefully one strives to be discreet. I'd hate to imagine what Kitty and Adele would say should they catch even the tiniest hint. As much as I like your friends, they do tend to talk behind one's back, don't they? And cut people dead for infractions they find too distasteful to tolerate, such as sexual trysts in the tough rough beyond the fourteenth green or variations on bestiality in the equipment shed."

She drained the glass and leaned back to study him. "How would they hear ridiculous crap like that?"

"You know how everyone gossips at the club, my darling. Why, if you were to overhear some of the things said in the men's locker room on a Saturday afternoon, you'd realize that one idle remark might become a full-grown scandal by that same evening. If you don't believe me, you might ask your father. He dearly enjoys playing gin rummy and swapping stories with his cronies. By the way, he and I are playing in the four-ball this weekend, both afternoons."

"Where's the damn cabin?"

Jay Jay did admire anyone with the aplomb to concede gracefully. He began to describe the wooded mountainside and the peaceful isolation they could look forward to. Mentally, he checked off the first potential hurdle. It had been cleared with several inches to spare.

"This is a town?" Corkie said, her voice laden with contempt. She flipped a cigarette out the car window and sank back in the seat, her eyes hidden behind sunglasses. "What do they do for excitement around here—watch the stoplight change from green to red?"

"It is a rather backward place," Jay Jay admitted. In fact, it was the most backward place he had been able to locate that met the vital criteria. It possessed no tourist attractions, no spectacular scenery, no mediocre scenery, no daily newspaper, no seasonal influx of outsiders. The locals had refused to discuss certain past events with the national press, presumably because they placed more value on their privacy than on the dubious rewards of five minutes of fame. It fit into the plan perfectly.

"Look at those hideous buildings, and those hideous yokels on the benches in front of them," his wife continued in the same contemptuous voice. "They're living proof that incest exists in the twentieth century. This whole idea is increasingly ridiculous, Jay Jay." She turned to offer him a smile, although he could see the effort it took. She had drained the contents of the flask more than an hour ago, and her tongue kept exploring her mottled lipstick in search of a stray drop. "A month out here with no one but those people will drive both of us absolutely crazy. Let's get the hell out of here. I swear I'll give up golf. I won't even have lunch at the club with my friends. I'll stay home and learn to cook. We can have a dinner party."

"Oh, but we both know that with a couple of martinis under your belt, you'd find yourself romping in the rough before too long, and we don't want that to happen. Your father would never forgive you if he learned about that . . . relationship." Jay Jay braked to a stop in front of a shabby grocery store and reached across the seat to pat her knee. "Borwaski's hardly up to your usual standards. What is the attraction?"

"You couldn't possibly understand it. He has a primitive charm, and a divine spontaneity. That sort of lust is a refreshing change from twice a week in the missionary position, year after tedious year. Afterwards, a kind word and a pat on the head satisfy him. A diamond in the rough, so to speak, and an amusing divertissement." After several unsuccessful attempts, she managed to light another cigarette. "I really don't want to linger in this dreadful town any longer than necessary. Get whatever it is and let's get out of here. I'm dying for a drink, even if I get it in the middle of some godawful woods and have to stir it with a twig."

17

"I put two cases of gin on the list. I'll unload them as soon as we arrive at the cabin, and you'll be sipping a martini on the deck before sunset. I made arrangements for the key to be left here with the owner of this little store. You wait here, my darling; I'll only be a minute or two."

"God, I hope so," she muttered through a cloud of smoke.

Once inside the store, Jay Jay spotted a grizzled man in overalls, with a faded cap covering tufts of white hair. He could not have envisioned a more perfect character for this, the next scene in his play.

"Anderson, for the Woodybrook Lodge key," he said, radiating what he hoped was a boyish enthusiasm.

"Whilkes. The man at the realty office dropped off the key a couple days back. You got everything you need? It's a far piece from town, and the road's a mess from the spring floods."

"We chose it for that very reason. I want to do some writing, and my wife just wants to relax for a few weeks. She's a little nervous about the isolation, however. You know how women can be about that."

"Can't say I do." Whilkes took a key out of a drawer and put it on the counter. "That all?"

Wishing he had a more garrulous character, but confident that he would make his point eventually, Jay Jay persisted. "Women worry about every little thing, especially one like my wife whose idea of a wilderness adventure is to search for a golf ball in the rough. She has all these crazy ideas about monsters lurking in the forest, prepared to jump out and grab her."

"Does she now?" the man said without interest.

"She sure does. She read some crazy story in the newspaper about how there was a really weird creature in this area—a big hairy monster with oversized feet. The tabloids refer to that sort of creature as 'Big Foot.' I told her that was the silliest thing I'd ever heard, but she keeps mentioning it."

"Does she now?" The storekeeper crossed his arms and regarded Jay Jay through flat, concrete-colored eyes.

Jay Jay resisted an urge to throttle the old man until the buttons popped off his ratty overalls, if only to elicit a response of any kind whatsoever. "Have you heard any of these fantastic rumors about monsters in the woods around here?"

"Yep."

"You have? Well, between the two of us, we know they're nonsense, but don't say a word to my wife." With a comradely wink, Jay Jay turned away, took a step, delicately faltered, and then came back to the counter. "They are nonsense, aren't they? I don't want to drag my wife out into the middle of the woods if there is some sort of monster skulking around. I love her too much to put her in danger just for the luxury of a few weeks of peace and quiet."

"Ebbers claims he saw something a while back. Ain't no reason to trust the ravings of an old sot. Bunch of kids out camping reported something, but everybody knew they took more beer coolers than they did hot dog buns."

"What did they claim to see?" Jay Jay demanded in a breathless voice.

"Big Foot. But there ain't no such thing. Sure you don't need any supplies?"

"Not a thing. Before we left town, I made a list." Jay Jay kept a faintly worried expression on his face as he walked out of the store. When he reached the car, he stopped and gnawed his lip as he gazed down the highway at a battered blue pickup, a scattering of mean houses, and the stoplight swaying in the breeze. As he glanced back at the store, he was pleased to see the storekeeper watching him through the screened door. Watching, no doubt, a husband unhappily considering the possibility that his beloved wife might be in danger from Big Foot.

Which she was.

He waited a week before returning to the store. He banged open the screened door and stomped to the counter. "Where's the sheriff's office?"

Whilkes put down a clipboard and shrugged. "Other side of the county. Good twenty miles."

"You got a telephone?"

"Yep." He picked up the clipboard and turned back to count a row of canned green beans.

Jay Jay allowed a hint of contrition to enter his voice. "Hey, I didn't mean to sound curt."

"Didn't notice."

"The problem is," Jay Jay continued stoically, "my wife saw someone looking through our bedroom window last night. I'm not going to let some local Peeping Tom frighten my wife."

"That so?"

"She was so startled that she wasn't sure. In fact, she was whimpering about how she saw some seven-foot-tall monster, but she was darn near hysterical and I figured she was imagining things. But I intend to call the sheriff and report this pervert. They've probably got a file on the guy already."

"They don't. No perverts around here for forty years."

Jay Jay put his fingertips on his temples and stared blankly at the floor. "That would explain . . ." he whispered, then broke off with a gulp. When the storekeeper merely scratched a number on the clipboard, he added, ". . . the footprints."

"Footprints?"

"I know it sounds bizarre, but this morning I went out to

the flower bed beneath the bedroom window and looked around. There were some marks in the mud that could have been footprints, if they hadn't been so oversized. They were twice as large as mine, and twice as deep. Whatever made those prints was bigger than any bear I've ever seen."

"That so?" The storekeeper totaled his figures and made a notation at the bottom of the clipboard. "You starting to believe in local fairy tales?"

"Hell, no," Jay Jay said, laughing at the very idea. He pulled out a grocery list and laid it on the counter. "My wife's a nervous city girl, that's all. It was just a shadow, or a branch rubbing against the window. There's no point in bothering the sheriff over something so trivial. Do you stock Perrier with lime?"

He waited only three days before his next visit to the store. This time he drove into town at a perilous speed and squealed to a stop in front of the store. A cloud of dust swirled in the sultry air as he banged through the door. "Can I use the telephone?"

"Yep." Whilkes pulled a black telephone from under the counter and set it down in front of Jay Jay.

"What's the sheriff's number?"

The man offered the number, then watched incuriously as Jay Jay called and sputtered the story of a perverted prowler who had been frightening his wife at the Woodybrook Lodge. After a series of incredulous barks and increasingly acidic responses, Jay Jay slammed down the receiver.

"They won't do a damn thing," he growled. "No investigation, no search party, no goddamn interest in catching this weirdo."

"Lots of timberland up that way."

"This joker doesn't seem to have much trouble with the

topography," Jay Jay said. His breath was ragged and his forehead creased by the ferocity of his scowl. He hit the counter with his fist, then looked down in surprise and slowly uncurled his white fingers. "He shows up almost every night to root through the garbage cans or slobber on the windows. My wife can't eat or sleep; she spends most of her time cowering inside, too frightened to go out in the yard or even sit on the porch."

"Take her home."

"She won't go. You know how stubborn women can be."

"Can't say I do."

"Well, they can be worse than mules. Corkie says she's not going to let this pervert ruin our vacation. She keeps reminding me that we paid for a full month, and by damn we're going to stay for a full month. If she were willing, I'd pack the car and we'd be heading back to the city within thirty minutes."

"Got a gun?"

"No," Jay Jay admitted, switching to a rueful tone, "and I couldn't shoot a rabbit, anyway. I have a thing about blood; it makes me queasy just to think about it." He paced across the worn wooden floor for several minutes, waiting for Whilkes to offer any further pearls of advice. "Tell me the truth," he finally said. "Several days ago you said there weren't any Peeping Toms in the area, but I've got evidence that someone or something is prowling around the lodge. Every morning the trash cans are overturned and there are muddy smudges on the porch. The flowers in the beds below the windows have been trampled into the ground. There are scratch marks on the screens. What's doing it?"

"Might be a bear," Whilkes said. "Been around here before."

Jay Jay stared at the man, then broke into a smile. "You're

probably right, Whilkes. It's just some hungry black bear sniffing around the lodge for food. As for the face in the window . . . well, my wife has a few emotional problems and does tend to allow her imagination to run wild. We're both used to city noises; the country noises seem louder than all the horns and buses and garbage trucks."

"Do they?"

"Yep." Jay Jay went out the door and paused by his car to gaze distractedly at the highway. The blue pickup was parked near an intersection. A child wandered along the shoulder of the road, squatting occasionally to extract an aluminum can from the weeds. A dog moved across the pavement, stopping in certain safety to sniff the worn yellow line. More interestingly, dark clouds gathered in the western sky, and as he watched, lightning flickered down at a distant target.

A dark and stormy night. It would provide a perfect background for the next stage of the plan.

Jay Jay drove back to the cabin and murdered his wife.

"My God! Someone help me!" he cried as he stumbled into the store and clutched the edge of the counter. Outside the rain pounded the empty highway, while lightning snaked across the sky and thunder boomed and reverberated. Jay Jay's clothes and hair were drenched; his face was streaked with a mixture of rain and tears. The back of his shirt was stained pink by blood that oozed from an open wound on his head. He beat his fist on the counter. "Whilkes, get out here! Call the sheriff, damn it! Someone has to help me!"

"Got trouble?" Whilkes said, appearing from behind a curtained doorway.

"Trouble?" Jay Jay repeated with a wild laugh. "Yeah, I've got trouble. This—this monster broke into the cabin. I only got a quick glimpse of him before he slammed me against the wall, but I've never seen such a horrible thing. Ugly, foul-smelling, yellow-eyes, covered with matted fur. Inhuman noises. God, I thought it was a nightmare. God . . ." His knees buckled and he grabbed the top of the cash register to hold himself up. "Don't just stand there and gape at me. Call the police—the sheriff—somebody!"

"Don't know what to say."

Jay Jay covered his face with his hands. His shoulders twitched as a strangled groan fought its way through his fingers. Abruptly he jerked his hands away and leaned across the counter to clutch the front of Whilkes's overalls. "Don't you understand what I'm saying, man? Big Foot stole my wife! You've got to get help."

"You don't say." The storekeeper took the telephone from under the counter and dialed a number. Once he had made it through a few preliminary remarks, he repeated Jay Jay's story to the sheriff. In the middle of what seemed an interminable length of time, Jay Jay's knees finally betrayed him and he sank to the wooden floor to lean against the counter. In that his face was not visible, he permitted one brief smile before resuming the bewildered, heart-broken expression of a recent widower.

For the next forty-eight hours, deputies swarmed through the woods in search of footprints. To everyone's regret, the steady rainfall had washed away all but a few deep indentations in the mud around the lodge. It had washed away any scent the dogs might have been able to follow, although the lodge was still tainted by a acrid odor of sulfur and wet fur. The broken window in the living room did little to protect Jay Jay and the sheriff from gusts of wind and splatters of rain as they stood in the middle of the room, conversing in low voices.

24

"Don't know what to tell you," the sheriff said, not for the first time.

Jay Jay hung his head, and in a dull voice said, "It's a nightmare. I'm going to wake up any second and find my wife asleep next to me in our bed. This doesn't really happen. I don't believe in monsters any more than I do in fairies and leprechauns. It had to be a bear or some animal like that, not some fantastical half-human creature from a B-grade science fiction movie." He looked up with a pleading smile. "Please, tell me I'm crazy. Tell me that I'm hallucinating and all I need is a few months in a padded room. Tell me that Corkie's safe."

"I wish I could, but something sure busted in here," the sheriff said, putting his hand on the despondent husband's quivering shoulder. "It did a helluva lot of damage to the room, and it must have smelled worse than a pile of ripe compost. Those smears of mud were made by damn big feet. We found traces of your wife's blood on the floor where she fought back. We've just got to pray she managed to escape and is trying to make her way out of the woods."

"It's my fault. When the rain eased up late that afternoon, I decided to walk down to the end of the road and check the mailbox for a letter from my publisher. I told Corkie to lock the door and stay inside until I got back. I couldn't have been gone more than thirty minutes at the most. I shouldn't have left her alone. It's all my fault."

"You can't keep blaming yourself for what happened, Mr. Anderson. You've got to get hold of yourself."

"Then find my wife, dammit! She didn't break the window, or ransack the room, or throw me against the wall as if I were a rag doll, or cut her finger to splatter blood on the floor. That creature has her. Find her before he does—he does something terrible to her! She's my wife, for God's sake." He turned away to rub his eyes. "My wife."

"Every man I've got is still out there in the woods," the sheriff said soothingly. "They're searching for any trail, any mark in the mud, any indication where this . . . thing might have gone. All we can do is pray that your wife is all right for the moment."

"What about caves? When Corkie saw this monster earlier, she said it resembled some sort of bear or gorilla. Wouldn't it be likely to hide out in a cave?"

The sheriff sighed. "One of the search parties found a cave not too far from here. There was a pile of garbage, mostly rusty cans and scraps of vegetable matter that might have been stolen from cans behind the lodge. They said there was a definite odor that was similar to what's here." He paused for a moment. "I didn't tell you this earlier, but the boys found a few bones in the back of the cave. Animals, of course. We sent them to the lab, but we're fairly sure they're rabbit, squirrel, maybe possum."

"You've got to find Corkie." Groaning, Jay Jay stumbled to the sofa and collapsed, his arm flung across his face to hide any hint of calculation. The next step was vital. "I don't think I can face the reporters," he added in a hoarse mumble. "They'll splash this across the top of every newspaper and trashy tabloid in the country. No one will believe it, of course—I don't believe it myself. But an army of them will descend on us. They'll stomp around the woods with television cameras. If this horrible creature is out there, he'll panic and flee so far into the mountains that you'll never find him . . . or my wife."

The sheriff came across the room and looked down with a frown. "You're right about that, Mr. Anderson. You and I know that something strange happened in this cabin, but when the press finishes with us, we'll be the biggest fools in the whole damn country. We had a problem like this a while

26

back, and the reporters came in like a flock of vultures to ridicule us. Damn tourists came in by the busload to picnic in the woods and scatter beer cans all over the place. Knocked on doors, took photographs of anyone foolish enough to step outside. No one in these parts likes publicity; we live here because we prefer nice quiet lives without outsiders bothering us."

"Is there any way to keep this out of the newspapers?" Jay Jay asked with a glint of optimism. "In the official reports could you just say Corkie wandered away from the cabin and lost her way?"

"Your wife's the only one who actually got a good look at this so-called Big Foot, and she never filed an official report." The sheriff tugged at his collar and gazed over Jay Jay's head at a watercolor on the wall. "We did find quite a few empty liquor bottles in the trash can out back. If your wife had a drinking problem, she might have decided to take a walk and lost her way. It'd be easy to get turned around out there."

"Thanks," Jay Jay said with a sincerely grateful smile. "But, please—find my wife."

Six days after the fact, the local weekly paper reported that Charlotte ("Corkie") McNevins Anderson, daughter of a well-known financial figure and wife of Jonathon Jerome ("Jay Jay") Anderson, had wandered into the woods and was still missing after an ongoing, intensive search by area lawmen. Jay Jay admitted privately to the reporter that his wife had a small drinking problem, and was pleased when his off-the-record comment was printed verbatim.

Due to the prominence of her maiden name, the national press picked it up, albeit more than a week after the incident. Jay Jay was not surprised when the sheriff, his men, and the few residents of the town all refused to discuss the incident with outsiders. He himself stayed locked in the cabin, keeping away from the windows and ignoring questions hurled through the door. The reporters eventually accepted the fact that there would be no lurid interviews with the grieving widower and drifted away to find other "human interest" stories. "Big Foot Stole My Wife" warranted headlines; "Aged Debutant Wanders Off in Drunken Daze" warranted only a sprinkling of paragraphs on back pages.

Fixing himself a glass of Perrier, Jay Jay sat down at the pine table and studied the piece of paper with the neatly printed list of steps in the plan. Most of them he checked off, the scratch of his pen accompanied by fleeting smiles. Corkie's father would have to be dealt with at some point in the future, but Jay Jay felt confident he could win the old man over with copies of the official police reports and the story in the local paper. If necessary, he was prepared to mention Borwaski's name. In any case, they could console each other over gin rummy in the locker room. He put a mark next to the old man's name with a notation to suggest a reward for any information leading to poor Corkie's whereabouts. It was time to taper off the trips to the grocery store to make hysterical calls to the sheriff's office. One more day in the cabin, and he could announce that he could no longer bear to stay there in painful expectation that his beloved wife might come stumbling out of the woods. He made a note to stress his growing depression when he told the sheriff he intended to return home. And to beg the sheriff to call collect if a single clue were found.

Only one major step remained on the list. With a flourish, Jay Jay checked it off, folded up the paper, and locked the list away in his briefcase. Everything else had been covered. The battered milkcan in the shed, perfect for indentations in the mud, had been rinsed off and replaced in its proper location.

The sodden fur coat would serve quite nicely as an odoriferous shroud. The aroma of rotten eggs had come from a bottle, which had been washed and placed beside the sink to dry before the sheriff had first raced up the driveway. The bones in the cave were a fortuitous discovery on the search party's part, and they had served to enhance the fantasy of a feral monster hunkered in a cave, ravaging his little forest friends and desperate to steal a she-woman for unspeakable purposes.

If he could have arranged such a scenario, it would have been appropriate, Jay Jay told himself as he changed into heavy jeans and a work shirt in anticipation of his final step. Anyone who allowed herself to seek pleasure with someone as crude as Borwaski deserved a lifetime with a truly crude Big Foot. Dinner parties of raw rabbit legs and stagnant water. Brilliant conversation consisting of grunts and belches. Brutally violent sexual encounters.

"If only I could have actually found the chap for you, my dear," Jay Jay said, savoring the irony of his vision. He went to the shed to get a shovel, then went around to his car parked in front of the lodge. The body was in the trunk, wrapped in the moldering fur, and then, for hygienic purposes, in a sturdy plastic storage bag, courtesy of the furrier. The sheriff and his men had searched every inch of the cabin and its immediate surroundings, but they had given the car only a cursory glance to see if Corkie might be propped in the passenger's seat.

He made a mental note to purchase a box of air freshener as he took out the body bag and slung it over his shoulder. With his free hand, he closed the trunk, then went back around the house to follow the path he'd chosen several months ago when he'd first scouted the terrain. The weeds tore at his trousers, but he had made sure there were no loose rocks to cause a fall, keenly aware that a broken leg would present a serious disruption of the plan. He reached the dreary little clearing that met all the specifications for a final resting place, dropped the bag without ceremony, and bent down to study the sodden leaves that carpeted the ground.

A deputy had ground a cigarette butt into the dirt, but there were no other signs anyone had visited the spot since the rain had stopped a week ago. Nor would anyone visit for many months to come, since the lodge was left vacant for the winter season. Jay Jay had made sure of that before he'd signed the rental agreement. Rain, sleet, and snow would eradicate any evidence the earth had ever been disturbed. By spring, weeds would burst through the leaves and grow waist-high by the time any nature lover or bird fancier ventured into the area.

"I must admit it was a perfect plan," Jay Jay said aloud, allowing himself a moment of glorious satisfaction for a well prepared plan that had come to such a satisfactory conclusion. It came, he thought smugly, of analyzing each and every detail, of noting the necessary steps, of determining how best to proceed, and then having the nerve to throw himself into the plan with the utmost confidence in his ability. He'd considered every possible variation and devised a way to deal with it. It therefore had worked perfectly.

"You preferred spontaneity, my dear?" he said to the lumpy form inside the plastic wrapper. "If time permits, I'll let myself go wild and do a dance on your grave. Would that please you, my darling?"

He put on gloves to protect his hands from any suspicious blisters, then drew a rectangle in the dirt and began to dig the grave. The top layer of dirt was carefully removed intact so that it could be replaced. With an allowance for erosion, the hole needed to be four feet deep. At approximately one foot per hour, he would be finished with his task and back at the cabin before dark. There he would savor the meal he'd prepared earlier, read in front of the fire, and finish packing for his trip home. He'd already made a list of those whom he would call immediately to relate the tragedy, and those who could wait a few days. A memorial service might be a nice touch. He added a note to his mental list to ask his secretary for help with the arrangements. She was still young enough to have a child or two, and he felt confident she was a superior cook and hostess.

As Jay Jay paused to blot his forehead with his handkerchief, he heard a crackle from the brush. It was followed by a rumbling noise, indistinct but ominously nearby. He tightened his grip on the handle of the shovel and stared at the impenetrable tangle of branches, scraggly brush, and stunted, misshapen pine trees. He saw nothing.

He again blotted his forehead, then returned to his labor. A second crackle sounded louder than a firecracker. Jay Jay dropped the shovel and spun around to study the undergrowth for any sign of movement. Nothing. He held his breath and strained to hear another crackle, but heard only a few distant birds and the droning of an airplane somewhere beyond the mountain.

Reminding himself that he needed to keep to his schedule in order to be back at the cabin at the allotted time, he once again began to jab his shovel into the yielding earth. One foot per hour. Four hours. There was no time for delays resulting from imagined noises.

Suddenly, the brush exploded behind him. A great weight slammed against Jay Jay's back. Ragged claws slashed his face. His nostrils stung with a putrid smell more devastating than nerve gas. His eyes watered, the tears mingling with rivulets of blood. Growls and snarls pounded his eardrums.

Muscular arms tightened around his throat until all he could do was croak in terror.

He staggered forward, then sprawled into the shallow grave, the weight on top of him driving his face into the mud. It filled his·mouth and nose, threatening to suffocate him. The snarls intensified as he struggled to push himself free. His hands scrabbled for the shovel but found nothing to use to fight off his attacker. The mud blocked his throat as he tried to scream. His fingers tore at the hairy arms that were wound around his neck more tightly than steel bands.

As he began to lose consciousness, he managed to free his face for a brief second. An inhuman howl swirled about him, a primitive proclamation of a successful kill. His eyes clouded with speckles of red, and his lungs began to burn. His head dropped back into the mud. In his final flicker of life, Jay Jay Anderson realized there was one small detail he had failed to include on his meticulous list. In his next life, he vowed, he would have to plan more carefully.

Paper Trail

Wellington House
#1 Wellington Road
Hampser, NC 27444

November 13, 1972

The Hampser Hero
c/o Hampser High School
Hampser, NC 27444

To the faculty adviser:

Congratulations on your ranking in the national contest for high school journals. How exceedingly proud of your young men and women you must be! All I can say is "Bravo!" These days so many young people are obsessed with athletics, politics, and other less admirable pursuits. To have such a dedicated and talented group must bring you vast satisfaction.

I shall assume that you are aware of my novels published under the pseudonyms of Alisha Wells and Alexandra Worthington. I would be delighted to speak to your classes. Wellington House can be rather lonely at times, and I truly look forward to each and every opportunity to visit with my fans and discuss my work. I cannot begin to count the number of times I've presented talks at luncheons—and loved every bite of it!

Perhaps I take advantage of my position in the literary community when I make this modest proposal, but I think you will agree it offers a splendid opportunity for one of your students. My filing has simply gotten away from me, as if it were a freight train barreling through the door each and every day. I put away one paper, and three more arrive in the post! If it weren't so aggravating, it would be amusing. But what with my editors calling, the publicity demands, and the necessity of responding to an increasing amount of fan mail, I can hardly find the time to write.

I would be so deeply grateful if you could recommend a student to come in for an hour or two a week and help me conquer this quagmire of paperwork. I regret that I can pay only minimum wage, but I hope one of your students who aspires to become an author might find it interesting to deal with my busy work. I would prefer a young woman, especially one who needs financial help and will appreciate any guidance I can give her in her future career. Please call me at your convenience.

Yours truly,
Aurora Wellington

T'was the night before Christmas
Or the week before, anyway

Dear Heather,

You are going to die when I tell you this! I mean, you'd better sit down before you read one more word! I am working for Aurora Wellington, who just happens to be Alisha Wells *and*

Alexandra Worthington. Are you dead??? I was so excited when you sent me *The Willow Lake Legacy* for my birthday that I finished it that very night. Then last month Miss Hayes gets this letter from her, and she wants somebody to file papers for her, and Miss Hayes asks me if I want to, and I just about faint! Do I want to work for Aurora Wellington? That's like asking me if I wanna marry Paul McCartney—right?

Hayes is waiting, so I say I might if the hours are right, and she says well, if you're not interested I'll speak to Rebecca Lawson, and I say maybe I'll ask my mother and it might be okay (Ma's the same and no, Dad hasn't written, but I figure it's hard to find stamps in prison). Anyway, I say yeah, and she gives me a letter that's *actually* from Aurora Wellington and tells me to go to her house (!!!) Saturday morning at ten.

I put on my blue jumper and the super shirt you gave me for Christmas last year, but I'm about to wet my pants when I ring the bell. She's written—what? forty books?—and I'm standing on her porch, ringing her bell like I'm a Girl Scout selling cookies. Finally, she answers the door, and is she beautiful! Think about it—how would you expect her to look? She's old, sure, but she has ash blond hair to her shoulders, deep lavender eyes like Elizabeth Taylor, and she's wearing—get this—a peignoir that's the exact same shade as her eyes. She's got to be at least fifty, but her complexion's right off the cover of *Seventeen*. She wouldn't make cheerleader—but who wants to be a dumb cheerleader when you can make zillions of dollars writing steamy novels?

My knees are knocking, but I manage to stammer my name and before I know it, we're sitting in the "parlor," as she calls it, me with a Coke and her with gin, and she's telling me (your humble second cousin!) her problems. Since I doubt Paul McCartney's going to call (for the record, Charlie and I broke up, so he's not calling either), I figure I've been snatched straight up to heaven. She tells me how she cannot concentrate on her "work" with all the paperwork lying around to depress her, and she wants me to come in for three hours on Saturday mornings and help out.

So for the last three Saturdays your cousin, the one and only greatest soon-to-be world-famous novelist, drops by the home of Aurora Wellington and reads her mail. Officially, I'm getting paid for three hours, but she comes in to chat and somehow it turns into four or five. Last week she had me do her grocery shopping on top of everything else, and I was so hungry I ate one of her apples on the way back from the store. If you'd like further details, you owe me a letter.

> Eat your heart out,
> Kristy

> Wellington House
> #1 Wellington Road
> Hampser, NC 27444

> March 15, 1973

Friends of the Barport Library
101 Swinton Lane
Barport, NC 27031

Dear Miss Chart,

Miss Wellington is dreadfully sorry that she will be unable to speak at your luncheon next month, and has asked me to pass along her regrets. As you know, Miss Wellington has always felt nothing but the deepest respect for the public library system's dedication to literacy. Only her frantic writing schedule could deter her from the opportunity to express her gratitude for your good works in the community. She dearly hopes you will forgive her when you read *Devilish Delights* (by Alexandra Worthington) a year from now.

Yours truly,
Kristen Childers

March 23, 1973

Dear Miss Hayes,

I'm really sorry that I didn't have time to do the interview with the head of the creative writing department at the college. I know it's too late for excuses, but Miss Wellington is having me work all day on Saturdays and sometimes on Sundays, and my mother's in the hospital again. I promise that I'll do better and won't miss any deadlines.

Sorry,
Kristy C.

Wellington House
#1 Wellington Road
Hampser, NC 27444

May 3, 1973

Dear Tommie,

Your idea was absolutely brilliant! The girl isn't especially brilliant, but she is ever so diligent and such a perfectionist that at times I want to throw my hands in the air and give up the ghost. The child can be dictatorial, if you can believe it—I'm almost afraid to open my mail, read it, and lay it down somewhere in my office, because along will come grim little Kristy, the incriminating evidence clutched in her sweaty hand, demanding to know if I've lost the envelope with the return address or gone completely batty and responded without consulting her! Consulting her, mind you! I'm old enough to be . . . her big sister, not to mention being a best-selling author (did you see the divine review in *Heartbeat Digest* last week?), and I'm being ordered about by a sweet young snippet who's not yet graduated from high school.

I know, I'm being utterly absurd. Now that I've trained her, why shouldn't I allow her to take complete control of the tedium so that I can take advantage of all the lovely free time to write, write, write—and meet the next nasty deadline? Yes, Tommie darling, I'm well aware that the book's due in less than a month and that daft young adolescent in publicity is putting together the tour. If you were more of a friend and less of a slave driver, you'd absolutely insist they put me up at the Plaza this year.

Huggies,
Aurora Borealis

A midsummer night's eve (maybe)

Dear Cuz,

I am absolutely pea green jealous about you going to Chapel Hill! There'll be so many gorgeous men that you won't have time to study, much less to "pursue a degree in political history." Try to think fondly of me as you take a toke (just joking!!!).

The junior college will have to do until I find a bag of money on the street. Ma's back at the butterfly farm (a.k.a. the rehab center), as I'm sure Aunt Sissie has told you, and her health insurance has run out. Miss W. is letting me work every day for a few hours, but I'm barely scraping by. I'd ask Dad, but I think he earns about ten cents an hour making license plates. He sent me a box of stationery for graduation. I hear you got a car, you lucky dog. Want a personalized plate? I know where to get one—ha ha.

Yeah, I'd like to hit up Miss W. for a raise, but writers don't make as much money as you'd think and she has a pretty quiet life. Nobody ever comes by, as far as I can tell, and she doesn't do anything except write all day and brood all night. She got mad at her agent because of some silly thing, and changed her telephone number, so now it's unlisted. I may be the only person on the planet who can call her. And, boy, did I learn my lesson last week! On the way to her house, I had a flat tire, and by the time I got it changed, I was two hours late. She about had a kitten, and made me promise to call whenever I'm going to be five minutes late. Remember that crazy lady who lived next door to us the summer you came? Miss W. makes *her* look like a Junior League president!!!

Okay, I'm exaggerating—Miss W. doesn't own three-dozen cats. Just one, and it's a mangy, motheaten old thing named Lady Amberline after the heroine in *Sweet Surrender* (or vice versa). I wish the darn thing would surrender itself to a garbage truck! Every time I look at her, I get itchy, and I spray myself for fleas once a week.

Charlie joined the army and shipped out to some base in Texas. The night before he left, we went out to dinner at a fancy restaurant and had this really serious talk, but basically he wants me to stay home and knit socks for two years. I would have laughed in his face—had I not been so tired that it sounded like a super idea.

To answer your nosy questions: I snooped through Miss W.'s papers and she is fifty-seven years old! Can you believe it? In person she looks every bit as sleek as she does on her cover shot, even if it was taken at least twenty years ago. She's never been married, although she does drop dark hints about a lost love, and her only relative is some cousin in Tallahassee who occasionally calls or writes. No, she doesn't read anyone else's books, but she absolutely despises Veronica St. James and is forever making hysterically funny comments about her. The house is about a hundred years old, and not in great shape, but it's "the ancestral home" that she inherited from dear departed "Papa" back in the days of the dinosaurs. The living room's a shrine to her awards (lots of them!) and yes, her bed has pink satin sheets and a ruffly canopy.

So, days with Miss W. and nights without Charlie. Life's a bowl of cherries, and I'm in the pits!!

Love,
Kristy

Wellington House
#1 Wellington Road
Hampser, NC 27444

February 27, 1974

Darling Tommie,

I shall arrive at the Plaza around five in the afternoon on Friday. I would adore to allow you to take me to dinner, but the train does take quite a long time and I'm afraid I'll be utterly exhausted. Tell Natalie that I shall call upon her at eleven the next morning to discuss this latest travesty of a cover. No reader in her right mind would give it a second glance—much less buy it!

Kristy will stay at the house during my tour to feed Lady Amberline, collect the mail, water the plants, and fend off burglars. The girl is a dear thing and ever so courageous about her family situation, which has all the makings of a gothic horror story. I've told you about her mother, a pathetic alcoholic, and her father, a contemporary blackguard if ever there were one. He's currently in prison for burglary, assault, attempted homicide, and a host of other barbaric charges.

Several weeks ago I drove by her house, simply out of curiosity, and it's one of those quaint tract houses with a weedy yellow lawn, at least one broken window, a cluttered carport, a roof within minutes of collapsing, and located in a development called, of all things, Clover Creek. Dandelion Dump would be more fitting!

Kristy dropped out of college this semester, saying she was unable to pay her tuition. She mentioned that she'd applied at a local restaurant for the night shift, but I told her in no uncertain terms that I should not be comfortable employing someone who, if I may lapse into colloquialisms, slings hash. No greasy fingers on my correspondence, thank you! Although my budget is already stretched to its meager limit, I told her to plan to put in a full day's work five days a week until she is able to return to school.

I must tell you this, Tommie dear, but never ever breathe a word of it to her! She's been dating a local boy for several months, and with her mother unavailable, I felt that someone should take a maternal interest in the matter and assess the boy. She arranged for him to come to the house to pick her up one evening last week, and brought him into the parlor to meet me. For the occasion, he chose blue jeans, white socks, sneakers, and the sort of blue cotton shirt one associates with factory workers (and why not? It seems he works at a poultry processing establishment!). I said nothing, of course, but the next day I did tell Kristy that he seemed curiously inarticulate, unintelligent, and we laughed until we cried as I painted a vivid picture of his dreary, beery future as a line foreman of a merry little band of chicken pluckers. I do believe we'll see no more of that young man, thank God. Kristy's indispensable and I'm not about to allow her to elope with a moon-faced factory worker!

Anyway, darling, lunch at the Russian Tea Room on Saturday!

Your obedient servant,
Aurora

Wellington House
#1 Wellington Road
Hampser, NC 27444

March 15, 1974

Dear Mrs. Cathwright,

I regret to inform you that your services are no longer desired at Wellington House. I have reviewed the household accounts, and was tempted to bring to Miss Wellington's attention numerous questionable purchases from Maclay's Market, an establishment owned, I understand, by your brother-in-law.

However, I feel it best not to disturb Miss Wellington. Should you desire references, please contact me directly. Miss Wellington is much too preoccupied with her work to speak to

you in person or to communicate with you in any fashion whatsoever, but if you insist, I cannot promise that she will not file
charges. Enclosed is severance pay of two weeks.

Yours truly,
Kristen Childers

From the desk of Aurora Wellington
March 28, 1974

Dear Mrs. C.,

Kristy has told me of your sudden decision to retire and move
to Earlsville to be near your son and grandchildren. Although I
am devastated by the loss of your invaluable services after all
these years, I do understand your feelings. I don't know how I
shall survive without your chicken salad and flaky, sinfully rich
cream pies. You've spoiled me rotten for twenty years, you
wicked woman! Lady Amberline sends her fondest regards,
and does hope you'll send photographs of those darling babies.

Warmly,
Miss W.

Wellington House
#1 Wellington Road
Hampser, NC 27444

September 2, 1975

Dear Mrs. Harold Maron,

I still giggle every time I think of you being married! Doesn't it feel totally weird to have a new name after all these years? Harold looks divine in the photographs, you are radiant, and even our bratty little cousin Wendy is sweet (did she put thistles in the flower basket?). I'm sick I missed the wedding. Miss W. still hasn't recovered completely, and is doing most of her writing in bed these days. You'd think the doctors could figure out what's wrong after all those tests, but no one has any ideas and poor Miss W. often feels faint if she ventures downstairs. I helped her out to the garden yesterday and we sat in the gazebo all afternoon, her dictating (and drinking gin, of course) and me scribbling until I thought my fingers would bleed. *The Scarlet Sand*, for your information, a Worthington book. It's going to be super—and after the disappointing sales figures for *The Passages of Pleasure*, it'd better be.

Did Mrs. Harold Maron come out of her honeymoon daze long enough to notice the return address? After the funeral, I went back to the house and found the sheriff howling on the doorstep. It seems my mother forgot to pay property taxes, and with the cost of the funeral and all the bills from the butterfly farm, there was no way I could catch up on the taxes and at the same time have electricity! Apparently, someone's already offered to buy it for back taxes.

I rented an okay apartment, but when Miss W. discovered it was on the wrong side of the tracks—in every sense of the word—she insisted that I move into the house. I figured I might as well, since she was keeping me until eight or nine o'clock every night, although my paycheck sure hasn't been reflecting the extra hours. Now at least I get room and board out of the deal. No satin sheets, alas. Just cat hairs on my pillow, Lady Amberline's cute way of reminding me of my allergies.

Love,
Sneezy

Wellington House
#1 Wellington Road
Hampser, NC 27444

May 29, 1976

Penman Publishing, Inc.
375 Hudson Street
New York, NY 10014
Miss Natalie Burlitzer, editor

Dear Miss Burlitzer,

Miss W. asked me to let you know that the manuscript of *Lady Amberline's Revenge* is within a few days of completion and should reach you by the end of next week. She's been working on it around the clock, and is sure you will be as delighted with it as she is.

Should you wish to discuss the manuscript, we will be at the lake house for the summer. There is no telephone, but the proprietor of the general store will convey messages, and I've been told you have his number. I look forward to meeting you this fall when we're in New York for the release of *The Sins of the Whittiers.*

Yours truly,
Kristen Childers

Banbury Cottage
RFD 1, Box 18
Willow Lake, NC 27019

July 25, 1976

Veronica, my dearest cohort,

I was so incredibly pleased for you when I saw that effervescent review in *Romantic Times*! If only the gal could have gotten the plot synopsis a bit less muddled—but we old hacks know how clumsy reviewers can be. I'm sure you laughed at that banal and ever so tacky line in paragraph four about "St. James's passion for convoluted prose," and also at the "stale predictability of the story." Then again, she did get the title right, and what else matters?

Although I'd intended to stay here until the end of August, we're heading back home tomorrow. Usually I can rely on total solitude at this end of the lake, but this year the cabin just down the road was rented to a trio of college boys . . . from Yale, I believe. There's certainly nothing Ivy League about them, let me tell you! They're forever thrashing and bellowing in the lake as if they were ungainly bears, and playing loud music until all hours of the night. One of them has cozied up to Kristy and lured her to their squalid parties, which no doubt degenerate into orgies of the most primitive and repulsive sort.

So I'm virtually getting no work done. Yesterday afternoon I ran out of typewriter paper, but Kristy was out in a battered rowboat with "her beau" and failed to return until after sunset. The beer on her breath was enough to make me quite ill to my stomach. She apologized as best she could, but

I told her to start packing at that very hour and not to leave the house under any circumstances. I can only hope they've failed to exchange addresses. What on earth will I do if he begins showing up at Wellington House?

Your number-one fan,
Aurora

Wellington House
#1 Wellington Road
Hampser, NC 27444

October 1, 1976

Wee Care Animal Clinic
454 Pathway Road
Hampser, NC 27444

Dear Dr. Wallsby,

Miss Wellington has asked me to express her gratitude for all the loving care you and your staff bestowed on Lady Amberline on that tragic day. We have searched the house from top to bottom, and can only conclude that Lady Amberline must have slipped out and chanced upon the poison in a neighbor's garden shed. After some consideration, Miss Wellington has decided that a new kitten would only cause her to grieve more deeply over Lady Amberline's untimely demise.

Sincerely,
Kristy Childers

Wellington House
#1 Wellington Road
Hampser, NC 27444

September 16, 1977

Dearest Tommie,

Kristy and I had a lovely summer at the lake house. This year there was no one to disturb us, and I was able to sit on the porch all day while Kristy tended to the chores and brought me trays at mealtime, always with a little vase of wildflowers. Once a tendril of poison ivy crept in, but I spotted it and Kristy nearly cried when she apologized, and so of course I forgave her. I know you think it's appallingly bucolic, but I get more writing done there in three months than I do the rest of the year. Whenever I need inspiration, I gaze out at the rippling azure water—and *voilà!* "Monica turned her azure eyes toward Dr. Bodley and the faintest hint of a smile rippled across her pale, worried face."

The visit was timely, I must admit. I had Kristy volunteer at the hospital last spring in order to glean some insights into the dynamics of the place. She became quite adept at sneaking into the emergency room to observe the gory casualties, and came home each evening with stories both charmingly lurid and screechingly funny. All I can say is I do not intend to be placed in one—ever.

The problems began with some shaggy young intern whom she took to meeting for coffee after his shift, and occasionally on his free days. One night she came home well after midnight, and it was obvious they had behaved indiscreetly. I said nothing, of course, but took it upon myself to have a word with the head of the program, one of Papa's old friends who should have retired decades ago! He was quite stuffy in his refusal to take action until I mentioned the possibility of an endowment for cancer research. Our young "Dr. Kildare" has decided to complete his internship at a hospital in California.

Don't think for an instant that I deserve to be scolded for interfering in Kristy's personal life. For one thing, the poor girl is technically an orphan and someone really and truly must watch out for her. If I allowed her to roam the streets when we're in New York, I have no doubt whatsoever she'd come back with someone sleazier than that convict father of hers. Her taste in men is atrocious, and without my constant supervision, she might well become the proverbial good time that was had by all!

I've encouraged her to attempt some writing of her own, but I fear it was an egregious error on my part. Only last week, she showed me the first chapter of a novel. I did my best not to laugh as I pointed out the weaknesses in her little story and the shallow characterizations.

I'm sending a snapshot of Pittypat, who simply appeared at the back door of the lake house one morning and refused to leave. I took one look at those big blue eyes and silky whiskers, and told Kristy to fetch a saucer of milk!

Your silly, softhearted author,
Aurora

Wellington House
#1 Wellington Road
Hampser, NC 27444

November 2, 1977

Wee Care Animal Clinic
454 Pathway Road
Hampser, NC 27444

Dear Dr. Wallsby,

Once again Miss Wellington has asked me to express her gratitude for your concern during the tragedy. I'm sure all of us are horrified that anyone could be so vicious as to strangle an innocent kitten and leave its poor little body in the gazebo. Miss Wellington was overwhelmed with shock when she found it, but she has finally recovered and is able to work.

Yours truly,
Kristen Childers

From the desk of Aurora Wellington
12-13-77

Dearest Veronica,

Yes, I think I will accept your kind invitation to spend a few days in Atlanta. The weather's as dreary as my thoughts (I did tell you about Pittypat, didn't I?), but I cherish the supposition that elegant luncheons, lavish dinner parties, and dedicated late night bouts of drinking and gossip will be my salvation.

It's so kind of you to consider Kristy. I must offer her regrets, alas. The deadline for the next Wells manuscript is coming up, and I've made so many revisions that she'll have to retype all six hundred pages during the holiday season.

See you in a week!

Wellington House
#1 Wellington Road
Hampser, NC 27444

January 6, 1978

Mrs. Janice O'Leod
1477 Lakeside Road
Tallahassee, FL 32304

Dear Mrs. O'Leod,

Miss Wellington apologizes for not writing herself, but the holiday season has thrown her off schedule and she is working frantically on her newest book. She asked me to let you know that she was delighted with the gloves and umbrella you sent her for Christmas, and hopes you enjoy the autographed copy of *The Sins of the Whittiers*.

I regret that I cannot give you our new unlisted telephone number, as per your request, but once it's been given to someone, it seems to spread like a virus until we're literally inundated with calls. I am under order to guard it as if it were a Vatican treasure.

As much as Miss Wellington would love to see you this spring, her dubious health dictates that she must decline your invitation to meet at your hotel for lunch. Due to time restraints, she is unable to entertain guests here at Wellington House.

Yours truly,
Kristen Childers

Wellington House
#1 Wellington Road
Hampser, NC 27444

September 18, 1983

Dear Traci,

I was thrilled to get your letter after all these years. I would have sold my soul to go to our tenth reunion, but Miss W. was so sick that there was no way to leave her for even an hour. She's had this problem for years, on and off, and it flares up at the most inopportune times. Did you hear why I wasn't at the fifth reunion? While I was getting dressed, I heard a noise and discovered Miss W. lying at the bottom of the stairs. It wasn't until the next day that I finally persuaded her to go to the emergency room for X-rays. Nothing broken, thank God, but she hobbled around with a cane for months.

My glamorous life? Get real—your carpools and baby-sitting crises and burned pot roasts sound a lot more exciting than what I do. You would not believe the amount of paperwork involved in being an author. It takes me all morning to sort through requests for personal appearances, send photographs to fans, respond to queries from the editorial and publicity departments, answer sweet little letters from junior high girls, and fend off supplications from "wannabee" writers who'd like Miss W. to critique their thousand-page manuscripts. Miss W. ordered me to fire the cook after an heirloom ring vanished, so I fix lunch and when the weather is nice, we eat in the gazebo. She dictates until it's too dark for me to see, and after I fix dinner, we spend our really "glamorous" evenings in the parlor. Miss W. can be somewhat funny when she's talking about some of her rivals, especially after she's been cooing on the telephone with them for hours.

I'm glad Heather saved the postcard from the Plaza, but the inside of the room's about all I see when we're there. Miss W. insists that I bring the portable typewriter and do revisions or work on the newsletter. Want to be on the mailing list so you'll know what Miss W. has for breakfast and what inspired her to write *Vanessa's Folly?*[*]

Enough of this dazzling lifestyle. So Charlie's getting bald, and his wife resembles a tugboat? Three children can do that. I almost threw up when I heard Sam Longspur's a dentist—I went out with him our junior year, and he spent so much time poking his tongue down my throat that I still get queasy just thinking about it. I knew Heather was pregnant, but I agree that I wouldn't have dared put on a bathing suit if I were such a blimp (don't you dare repeat that!).

I must stop. Miss W. wants me to pack for our annual jaunt to New York, where she will wine and dine with her editor and agent, and I will merely whine. Thanks so much for all the luscious gossip from the reunion. Maybe I'll make the next one and Charlie will be as bald as a persimmon.

Love,
Kristy

[*]An English muffin and tea, and have you ever read *The Roses in Eden* by Veronica St. James?

Wellington House
#1 Wellington Road
Hampser, NC 27444

November 10, 1984

Thomas Domingo Literary Agency
188 W. 79th Street
New York, NY 10122

Dear Mr. Domingo,

I have reviewed the royalty statements of 10/31/84 and have found serious discrepancies either in the publisher's computations or in yours. Please note return figures for *Summer of the Shadows* and the lack of information regarding foreign sales of same. Also, in that *Cape Serenity* has gone into a third printing, I find it curious that no sales are reported for the six-month period prior to the statement.

I am hesitant to bring this to Miss W.'s attention. For the last five years she has relied on me to handle all of her business affairs, and trusts me to do so with meticulous care. Frankly, she is unable to work more than three or four hours a day as it is. I cannot allow her to lose that precious time by concerning herself with financial matters.

Please respond to this within ten days.

Yours truly,
Kristen Childers

From the desk of Aurora Wellington

Tommie, dearest:

I am at a loss for words—after having written millions of them over the last twenty years! Apparently you are, too, in that you've failed to answer my last two letters. But if what Kristy has shown me proves to be true, then I can never forgive you. How many years have I trusted you? Now Kristy has told me that you have systematically stolen thousands and thousands of dollars from me. Tommie, dear Tommie, you must come down immediately after the holidays and review all this over a civilized glass of gin, not in the gazebo at this time of year, but surely in the parlor.

Yours in bewilderment,
Aurora

Wellington House
#1 Wellington Road
Hampser, NC 27444

December 10, 1984

NC State Correctional Facility
Raleigh, NC 27603
#1987-431-1

Dear Dad,

So they're letting you out after all these years, are they? I'm sure their rehabilitation efforts have taken effect and you will enter society determined to lead a blameless life. It must be hard to imagine yourself living on the outside, but let's hope you've had enough vocational training to find a job—even in these economically depressed days. I realize there's still a lot of discrimination against convicted felons, and it's really not fair to send you out onto the streets with only a few dollars and a new suit. Anyway, good luck job hunting and don't faint when you see how expensive everything is out here!

As you know, I live with an incredibly rich old woman who's written best-selling novels for thirty years. I hate to say it, but she'd be utterly helpless without me. She's small and frail and her hearing seems to get worse every year, but thank God her mind is quite sharp and she has a fantastic memory for details. She never forgets a face and can describe it with astonishing preciseness—as can all writers. On the other hand, she can't remember to put away her jewelry in the box on the dresser in her bedroom, and last week on her way to bed, she left the kitchen door ajar and the house was freezing by morning. We're lucky that she's too miserly to install decent locks; she's misplaced the keys so often that I've become quite adept with a hairpin. I guess that's one talent I inherited from you—ha, ha.

Anyway, I think I would like to see you, if only for old time's sake. The only two days I will not be available are December 24 and 25, when I'm visiting Cousin Heather for the first time in years. She has four kids now, and Harold is some kind of manager at his office. This time I've warned Miss W. that I am definitely going, even if she objects or claims to be sick. I'm hoping to be at Heather's by dark, and will be home the next evening. I feel terribly guilty about leaving Miss W. all alone in the house for two days, but our cleaning woman insists on being with her own family and no one else ever comes by to see Miss W. I don't really blame them; the house is so isolated at the end of the road, and you can't have neighbors if you own all the land for several miles. It's the only drawback I can think of to being rich!

Write me a note once you're settled. I'd tell you to call, but the squirrels have been gnawing on the telephone lines again and it usually takes several weeks for a repairman to come.

Your daughter,
Kristy

Wellington House
#1 Wellington Road
Hampser, NC 27444

April 11, 1985

Shady Oaks Realty, Inc.
3168 Katherine Avenue
Hampser, NC 27444

Dear Ms. Rowan,

Please address all future correspondence concerning the sale of Wellington House and the adjoining property to me, c/o Thomas Domingo Literary Agency, 188 West Seventy-ninth Street, New York, NY 10122. I'm sure you are aware of how lengthy a process probate can be, but I believe that we can entertain offers and perhaps work out a lease-purchase agreement until a sale can be finalized.

As for the house Miss Wellington owned in the Clover Creek addition, I have rented it to a distant member of my family and will allow him to occupy it at least until the estate is settled.

Should an emergency arise, I am staying at the Plaza and

you may leave a message at the desk. If the remodeling proceeds on schedule, as of the first of June I will be in permanent residence at the house on Willow Lake.

Yours truly,
Kristen Childers

Dear Suzanne,

I'm sorry it's taken so long for me to respond to your charming letter, but I must say I'm impressed with the dedication you've shown in discovering my real name and tracking me down at this address. I'm delighted that you enjoyed *Lady Amberline's Fortune*, and I agree that she's a feisty young woman with a strong sense of ambition. You might watch for *Shadows and Smoke*, a more contemporary novel about a girl just a few years older than you!

As for your generous offer, I fear I must demur. Although there are days that I feel as if I'm drowning in papers, I simply wouldn't be comfortable having someone come in to assist with the filing and correspondence. You sound like a sensible girl, perhaps as ambitious as Amberline, and I'm confident that you'll find a way to have a successful career in literature, just as I did.

Warm wishes,
Kristy Childers

Heptagon

"Miss Neige," I say, tactfully using the name she prefers, "please try to open up to me before our time is over. I can understand how difficult this must be for a young woman such as yourself, but we must talk about it."

"Are you bored, Doctor? I've been many things, but never bored. Shall I entertain you with a narrative of the murder?"

I struggle to reply in a neutral tone. "Let's go back just a bit. The information I was given has led me to think that your childhood was stressful."

"I think that might be too mild a description for the torment inflicted on me by my stepmother. My real mother killed herself when she found out that my father was unfaithful to her. He claimed she died of tuberculosis, but we know better."

"We?"

"You and I, Doctor." She settles back on the couch and puts her hands behind her neck, her elbows jutting sharply. From this angle I can see the nerves bunched in her neck like metal cables.

"In the mornings," she continues in an oddly detached voice, "I'm grumpy until I've had my coffee. She was always jabbering at me, pecking at me like a magpie. All I wanted was peace and quiet. There's nothing wrong with that, is there?"

"I shouldn't think so," I reply, writing the word "grumpy" in my notebook. It's a peculiar word coming from someone so young and well educated.

"She didn't agree, and was forever telling me that being grumpy wasn't attractive. She knew how much she annoyed me—which is exactly why she did it!"

I take a moment to answer. "Miss Neige, we're not here to decipher your stepmother's motives. You are what concerns us in this session. How did you feel when your stepmother said these things?"

Her lips twitch with repressed anger. "How do you think I felt? Do you expect me to say I was grateful? I assure you I was not. She criticized me continually, but always with such subtlety that my father never noticed. He would beam at her as if she were the most beautiful and generous person he'd ever met. There were times I wanted to slap the smile off his face and make him see what she was doing to my self-confidence with her sly digs about my appearance or lack of a social life."

"You lacked a social life? I would have thought an attractive young woman like yourself would have been surrounded by suitors."

"Then you would have been wrong. As a young child, I was bashful."

"You—bashful?" I say, making a note of the word.

"After my mother's death, I rarely spoke to anyone other than the household servants. Since I was taught by tutors, I had no opportunity to make friends. By the time I was twelve, I was bashful so much of the time that I was unable to engage in ordinary social interaction. Any persistent effort to force me to do so gave me hives that only bed rest and antihistamines could relieve. Oh, yes, I was bashful. She found that *très amusant*."

"You seem quite articulate," I say encouragingly.

"I'm not always bashful now," she says. "Despite her twisted pleasure in my disability, I eventually overcame it and made a few friends. She was quick to point out that my father's wealth and power were my two best attributes, but I refused to listen to her. I persuaded my father to give me a clothing allowance so she could no longer dress me in unflattering smocks and bulky sweaters."

I feel a distinctly unprofessional pang of sympathy for my patient. She has a lovely face, with luminous green eyes and a heart-shaped mouth. I have yet to see her smile, but I suspect she has even white teeth and a dimple. Her voice is so melodious I expect her to burst into song at any moment.

Aware that she is waiting for me to respond, I say, "It sounds as if your life improved at this point."

"Oh, yes, there were times when I was happy. When John Earl asked me to accompany him to the Harvest Ball, I was almost ecstatic. I bought a new dress and spent the day at the salon having a manicure, pedicure, and facial. The proprietor himself did my hair." She sits up and pushes her raven hair above her head in a sloppy cascade; I must admit the effect is beguiling. "While I was getting dressed for the ball, she came into my room and told me I looked like a prostitute. I replied that I was happy and that she was jealous of my youth and beauty. She pushed me, so I pushed her back. Before I realized what was happening, we were kicking and scratching each other, and our screams brought my father to the door."

"What did he do?" I ask softly.

"She began to cry and accused me of attacking her for no reason. My father chose to believe her filthy lies and ordered me to stay in my room for the rest of the night. John Earl was told on the doorstep that I'd changed my mind about going to the ball."

"You must have been disappointed."

"I certainly was no longer happy," she says with a trace of sarcasm. "I remained in my room for a month, refusing to go downstairs for meals. I was sleepy all of the time, as if I were under the influence of a hypnotic spell. My stepmother took to standing over the bed and telling me that I wasn't sleepy, but instead sluggish and self-indulgent. I couldn't help it, Doctor. Some mornings I'd force myself to get dressed, but then I'd realize I was sleepy and simply lie down on the bed."

"Do you think you might have been depressed?"

"I was sleepy, not depressed! Why can't you listen more carefully? My dreams became increasingly bizarre, until the line between fantasy and reality became blurred. Did John Earl really climb the wall to my bedroom window and plead with me to escape? Did my mother come into the room and tell me I could go to the ball if I'd wear her wedding dress? Maybe I'm sleepy now—and you're a figment from a nightmare! If I snap my fingers, will you vanish in a puff of smoke? Shall we find out, Doctor?"

Although our fifty minutes are up, I am reluctant to end the session while she's agitated. I excuse myself, go into the reception room, and tell my secretary that I'm going to continue the session and will lock up the office when I'm finished. Upon my return, I find Miss Neige sitting on the edge of the couch, her purse in her lap and her eyes red and watery.

"Would you care for a glass of water?" I ask her.

"No," she says curtly as she puts her purse on the floor and lies back.

I want to assure her that she is not the first patient to lose her composure on my couch, but I am leery of upsetting her with unwanted solicitude. "Well, then," I say as I resume my seat, "shall we continue, Miss Neige?"

"Where was I?"

"I believe you were discussing the period in your life when you were sleepy . . ."

"Or so I thought until one of the kitchen maids saw my stepmother putting a few drops of something in my morning coffee. The girl smuggled the vial to me, and I quickly determined that it contained an opiate. I hadn't been sleepy, Doctor—I'd been dopey as a result of her insidious scheme to further discredit me in my father's eyes. I gave the maid a few coins and asked her to replace the vial and say nothing."

"Dopey," I write in my notebook, circling it several times. Again, a strange choice of words for a sheltered young woman such as Miss Neige. I add "happy" and "sleepy." A pattern seems to be forming, as yet too indistinct for me to comprehend. "What did you do?" I ask.

"I poured the coffee out my window each morning and continued to lie in bed with a languid expression on my face. After a time, my system was cleansed and I was no longer dopey. She never realized, as she prowled around my room, that I was watching her. She tried on my jewelry and smoothed my skin creams on her wrinkled face as if they could transform her. If my father had seen her scowling into the mirror on the wall, he would have realized what an old hag she really was, but she'd poisoned his mind."

"Surely he would have been concerned if you'd told him about this opiate."

"She was much too shrewd," says Miss Neige. "Somehow she discovered that I'd learned of her scheme. She accused the kitchen maid of theft and fired her, then took the vial to my father and claimed that she'd found it in my room. She convinced him that I needed to be sent to a hospital to overcome my dependency. Before I could present my side of the story, I was taken from my home and placed in a room with barred windows and an iron cot. Sadistic nurses watched my every move through a slot in the door. Other patients pinched me until my arms were covered with welts and bruises. I was allowed one hour a day to walk on the grounds, always accompanied by an attendant with thick, flabby lips and an insolent smirk. Despite my revulsion, I feigned fondness for him and persuaded him to help me escape."

"That was very clever," I murmur.

"I thought so, until I ventured beyond the fence and realized I had nowhere to seek refuge. I was afraid to be seen walking along the road into town, so I went into the woods, hoping I might chance upon an abandoned dwelling in which I could take shelter. The attendant had provided me with enough food to survive for several days. As soon as the furor over my escape had abated, I could steal clothes off a line, disguise myself as a country girl, and seek employment in some menial capacity. It was hardly the life I'd envisioned as a child, but it was all I could think to do until my circumstances changed."

"Did you find such a dwelling?"

"I do believe my mouth is getting dry. May I please have a cup of water?"

I go into the reception room to ask my secretary to bring a carafe of cold water and glasses, but she has left for the day. As before, when I return, Miss Neige is upright and clutching her purse. I see on her face the steely expression that must have been there when she was fighting her way through the woods, determined at all costs to take control of her life.

I offer her a cup of water.

She snatches it out of my hand and greedily drinks. When the cup is empty she says, "Shall I continue?"

"Please take your time, Miss Neige."

"As the sunset faded, I came upon a small cabin situated

near a stream. There were no lights on inside or any indication that it was inhabited, yet I was leery of approaching. I
was taught to speak French and play the harpsichord, but
training in self-defense had never been included in my curric-
ulum. Neither had breaking and entering—but it's not nearly
as difficult as one might assume."

"And was the cabin empty?" I ask.

"Yes. It was very dark by then, and I had no candle or lan-
tern. I found a pile of filthy blankets in one corner. I made a
bed, ate some of the bread and cheese in my bag, and then
curled up and fell asleep of utter exhaustion."

"And the next morning?"

"I was able to take a better look at my temporary home.
The only furniture consisted of a crude, hand-hewn table and
two benches. Bits of crockery and cutlery were scattered on
the floor. I gathered them up and washed them in the stream,
then did the same with the blankets and hung them on
branches to dry. I spent the rest of the day whisking the floor
with a clump of weeds, scrubbing grime off the windowpanes,
and searching the woods for edible berries. I stayed near the
cabin in case I heard bloodhounds and needed to retrieve my
remaining food and flee once again. I never did, though, and
came to believe that when my father and stepmother were in-
formed of my escape, she convinced him it was for the best to
leave me out on my own. I'm quite sure she secretly hoped I
would be killed by a wild animal or expire from hypothermia.
She would have liked that. I could envision her standing by
my grave, weeping for my father's benefit while considering
which trinkets of jewelry to take from my dressing table
drawer."

I make a small noise meant to assure her that she has my
attention. "And . . . ?"

"I knew a diet of berries and water would not sustain me

much longer. The berries, in particular, made me sneezy. I was forced to rip up my slip for handkerchiefs."

"Berries made you sneezy?" I add the word to my growing list. "Isn't it more likely that you were allergic to mold inside the cabin?"

"Does it matter why I was sneezy?" she retorts with a sardonic smile. Contrary to my expectations, her teeth are as sharp as those of a fox.

"Please continue," I say, disconcerted.

"Only if you'll stop contradicting me. I do not care to be labeled by someone who knows so little about me. It's very rude, Doctor."

"My apologies, Miss Neige."

"And you understand that I was sneezy?"

"I'll record it in my notebook."

"All right, then. Keeping the cabin as a base, I commenced to explore in all directions until I found an isolated farmhouse several miles away. I stole potatoes and turnips from bins in the barn. A week later I returned, waited until the family left, and went into the house. I filled a pillowcase with candles, matches, packages of beans and rice, and a loaf of bread. I could have taken more, but it was vital that the residents remained unaware of my unauthorized visits."

"You went back several times?"

"Oh, yes, and also to other farmhouses I'd discovered. Often the houses were occupied, forcing me to rely on what I found in barns and outbuildings. But every now and then fortune smiled on me and I was able to return to my cabin with the makings of a veritable banquet. Who would have thought I'd make such a fine thief?"

It is not difficult to imagine her concealed by shadows, spying on farmers and their families. I make a noncommittal noise.

"Don't you agree, Doctor," she continues in an amused voice, "that someone of my breeding should be totally inept in basic survival skills?"

"Yes, indeed," I murmur, noticing that it's beginning to grow dark outside. I consider turning on my desk lamp, but decide to wait. "Perhaps we should move along, Miss Neige."

"As you wish."

I expect her to speak, but she gazes at the window. My tape recorder is whirring like an insect in a distant field, ready to capture our voices so I will be able to provide an accurate transcript to the prosecutor. I decide to venture into treacherous areas. "This must have been a lonely time, Miss Neige."

"But it wasn't, not at all," she says heatedly. "They began to arrive. First one, than another—each demanding a meal, a place to sleep, clothing. It was draining. I was obliged to become the nurturing figure, much as yourself. I was the doctor, the one who murmured much as you've been doing and encouraged them to relax. I had no choice. They insisted on calling me 'Doc' despite my protests."

"They?" I am bewildered. There is nothing in the police report to indicate there were other occupants at the scene of the crime.

"Yes!" she snaps. "The cabin became quite crowded. I was forced to scavenge for food several times a week to keep them fed. The blankets had to be washed every day. I would leave, and when I came back, find that the fire had been doused or the table overturned. Things had been peaceful before they came, and I begged them to go away."

"Why didn't you leave?" I ask.

Miss Neige jerks around and stares at me. "And go where? Back to the hospital? Back to my stepmother's home? I had no place to go—and I wasn't willing to abandon my idyllic little cabin simply because they were there. It was crowded, but not intolerable. It's not as if we were running into each other." Her laugh reminds me of the caustic echo of a crow. "How could we do that?"

"Who were 'they'?" I ask hesitantly.

"You are such a fool."

"I am?" I don't know how else to respond.

"Yes, you are. Why should you be surprised at the number of people living in my cabin in the woods? Is there a reason I should have been alone? Did I not deserve companionship and company? Am I as ugly as my stepmother says?"

"Dear, no," I say as I hastily stand up. "You are a charming young woman, and as I said, most attractive. I'm just not clear about the . . . arrangements at the cabin."

"The murder." She says this flatly. "That's what you want me to talk about."

"Would it be too painful to discuss?"

"No." Her voice rises in pitch. "That afternoon I was sleepy, so I went out by the stream to take a nap. I made myself a nice bed of pine branches, and was dreaming of servants and food on platters when he accosted me. I awoke to find his lips pressed against mine, his hands on my shoulders, his hair dangling in my face like a cobweb. Blinded by terror, I grabbed a stone and defended myself. Only when I came to my senses did I discover that it was poor John Earl sprawled on the ground, his skull crushed by my repeated blows. Before he died, he managed to tell me that he'd spent months searching for me, starting at the hospital and then questioning local farmers until he'd been able to narrow down the area."

"How distressing."

"An interesting word, Doctor. I murdered the only man who ever pretended that he loved me. I'm not sure he really did, considering my father's position. He might have. Then again, I didn't really murder him. I'd just been jolted out of a dream, and I suspect I was dopey. Dopey can be very unpleasant. Grumpy can, too, although he is rarely violent."

Her green eyes are flickering like strobe lights. Her expression shifts as quickly; a smile becomes a smirk and then a scowl. I begin to understand what thus far has sounded like a fairy tale of a little girl, a wicked stepmother, and a cozy cottage in the woods.

"Miss Neige," I say, "our time is up."

"Call me Blanche," she says as she picks up her purse and opens it, then stares at its contents with a curiously complaisant smile. "Bashful came up with the name. He was smitten with the French tutor, although he could never bring himself to confess his feelings to her. Poor, tongue-tied Bashful. Not even Doc could help him."

I clear my throat. "I think you're as aware of your condition as I am. You have what's known as multiple-personality syndrome. We can work together to help you find a way to balance these distinctive aspects of your—"

I stop because she's taking a knife out of her purse.

"There's one you haven't met, Doctor," she says in an insolent drawl. "Say hello to Nasty."

Make Yourselves at Home

It was the summer of her discontent. This particular moment on this particular morning had just become its zenith; its epiphany, if you will; its culmination of simmering animosity and precariously constrained urges to scream curses at the heavens while flinging herself off a precipice, presuming there was such a thing within five hundred miles. There was not. Florida is many things; one of them is flat.

Thus thwarted by geographical realities, Wilma Chadley could do no more than gaze sullenly out the kitchen window at the bleached grass and limp, dying shrubs. Fierce white sunlight baked the concrete patio. In one corner of the yard remained the stubbles of what had never been a flourishing vegetable garden, but merely an impotent endeavor to economize on groceries. Beyond the fence, tractor-trailers blustered down the interstate. Cars topped with luggage racks darted between them like brightly colored cockroaches. The motionless air was laden with noxious exhaust fumes and the miasma from the swampy expanse on the far side of the highway.

Wilma poured a glass of iced tea and sat down at the dinette to reread the letter for the fifth time since she'd taken it from the mailbox only half an hour ago. When she finished, her bony body quivered with resentment. Her breath came out in ragged grunts. A bead of sweat formed on the tip of her narrow nose, hung delicately, and then splattered on the page. More sweat trickled down the harshly angular creases of her face as the words blurred before her eyes.

From the living room she could hear the drone of the announcer's voice as he listed a batter's statistics. As usual, her husband, George, was sprawled on the recliner, drifting between the game and damp, uneasy naps, the fan whirring at his face, his sparse white hair plastered to his head. If she were to step between him and his precious game in order to read the letter, he would wait woodenly until she was done, then ask her to get him another beer. She had no doubt his response would be identical if she announced the house was on fire (although she was decidedly not in the mood to conduct whimsical experiments in behavioral psychology).

Finally, when she could no longer suffer in silence, she snatched the leash from a hook behind the door and tracked Popsie down in the bathroom, where he lay behind the toilet. "It's time for Popsie's lunchie walk," she said in a wheedling voice, aware that the obese and grizzled basset hound resented attempts to drag him away from the cool porcelain. "Come on, my sweetums," she continued, "and we'll have a nice walk and then a nice visit with our neighbor next door. Maybe she'll have a doggie biscuit just for you."

Popsie expressed his skepticism with a growl before wiggling further into the recess. Sighing, Wilma left him and went through the living room. George had not moved in over an hour, but she felt no optimism that she might be cashing a check from the life insurance company any time soon. Since his retirement from an insignificant managerial position at a factory five years ago, he had perfected the art of inertia. He could go for hours without saying a word, without turning his head when she entered the room, without so much as flickering when she spoke to him. He bathed irregularly, at best. In the infrequent instances in which she failed to harangue him, he donned sweat-stained clothes from the previous day. Only that morning he'd made a futile attempt to leave his dentures in the glass beside the bed, citing swollen gums. Wilma had made it clear that was not acceptable.

She headed for the house next door. It was indistinguishable from its neighbors, each being a flimsy box with three small bedrooms, one bathroom, a poorly arranged kitchen, and an airless living room. At some point in the distant past, the houses had been painted in an array of pastels, but by now the paint was gone and the weathered wood was uniformly drab. Some carports were empty, others filled with cartons of yellowed newspapers and broken appliances. There were no bicycles in the carports or toys scattered in the yards. Silver Beach was a retirement community. The nearest beach was twenty miles away. There may have been silverfish and silver fillings, but everything else was gray. During the day, the streets were empty. Cemetery salesmen stalked the sidewalks each evening, armed with glossy brochures and trustworthy faces.

Polly Simps was struggling with a warped screen as Wilma cut across the yard. She wore a housedress and slippers, and her brassy orange hair was wrapped around pink foam curlers. There was little reason to dress properly in Silver Beach since the air conditioner had broken down at the so-called clubhouse. For the last three years the building had been used solely by drug dealers and shaky old alcoholics with unshaven cheeks and unfocused eyes. Only a month ago a man of indeterminate age had been found in the empty swimming pool behind the clubhouse. The bloodstains were still visible on the cracked concrete.

"Damn this thing," Polly muttered in greeting. "I don't know why I bother. The mosquitoes get in all the same." She dropped the screen to scratch at one of the welts on her flabby, freckled arm. "Every year they seem to get bigger and hungrier. One of these days they're gonna carry me off to the swamp."

Wilma had no interest in anyone else's problems. "Listen to this," she said as she unfolded the letter. When she was done, she wadded it up, stuffed it in her pocket, and waited for a response from one of the very few residents of Silver Beach with whom she was on speaking terms. Back in Brooklyn, she wouldn't have bothered to share the time of day with the likes of someone as ignorant and opinionated as Polly Simps. That was then.

"I never heard of such a thing," Polly said at last. "The idea of allowing strangers into your own home is appalling. The fact that they're foreigners makes it all the worse. Who knows what kind of germs they might carry? I'd be obliged to boil the sheets and towels, and I'd feel funny every time I used my silverware."

"The point is that Jewel Jacoby and her sister spent three weeks in an apartment in Paris. Jewel was a bookkeeper just like I was, and I know for a fact her social security and pension checks can't add up to more than mine. Her husband passed away at least ten years ago. Whatever she gets as a widow can't be near as much as we get from George's retirement." Wilma rumbled in frustration as she considered Jewel's limited financial resources. "And she went to Paris in April for three weeks! You know where George and I went on vacation last year? Do you?"

Polly blinked nervously as she tried to think. "Did you and George take a vacation last year?"

"No," Wilma snapped, "and that's the issue. We talked

about driving across the country to visit Louisa and her loutish husband in Oregon, but George was afraid that the car wouldn't make it and we'd end up stranded in a Kansas cornfield. He's perfectly happy to sit in his chair and stare at that infernal television set. We've never once had a proper vacation. Now I get this letter from Jewel Jacoby about how she went to France and saw museums and cathedrals and drank coffee at sidewalk cafes. All it cost her was airfare and whatever she and her sister spent on groceries. It's not fair."

"But the French people stayed in her apartment," Polly countered. "They slept in her bed and used her things just like they owned them."

"While she slept in their bed and sat on their balcony, watching the boats on the Seine! I've never set foot in Europe, but Jewel had the time of her life—all because the French people agreed to this foolish exchange. I'll bet they were sorry. I've never been in Jewel's apartment, but she was the worst slob in the entire office. I'd be real surprised if her apartment wasn't filthier than a pig sty."

Polly held her peace while Wilma made further derogatory remarks about her ex-coworker back in Brooklyn. Wilma's tirades were infamous throughout Silver Beach. She'd been kicked out of the Wednesday bridge club after an especially eloquent one, and was rarely included in the occasional coffee-and-gossip sessions in someone's kitchen. It was just as well, since she was often the topic.

Wilma finally ran out of venom. Polly took a breath and said, "I still don't like the idea of foreigners in my house. What was the name of the organization?"

"Traveler's Vacation Exchange or something like that." Wilma took out the letter and forced herself to scan the pertinent paragraph. "She paid fifty dollars and sent in her ad in the fall. Then in January she got a catalog filled with other people's ads and letters started coming from all over Europe, and even one from Hawaii. She says she picked Paris because she'd taken French in high school forty years ago. What a stupid reason to make such an important decision! I must say I'm not surprised, though. Jewel was a very stupid woman, and no doubt still is."

Wilma went home and dedicated herself to making George utterly and totally miserable for the rest of the summer. Since she had had more than forty years of practice, this was not challenging.

Florida/Orlando X 3-6 wks 0
George & Wilma Chadley 2/0 A, 4, 2 GB
122 Palmetto Rd, Silver Beach FL 34101
97
97
(407) 521-7357
ac bb bc cf cl cs dr fi fn gd gg go hh mk ns o pk pl
pv ro rt sba se sk ss tv uz wa wf wm wv yd

"Here's one," Wilma said, jabbing her finger at an ad. "They live in a village called Cobbet, but it's only an hour away from London by train. They have three children and want to come to Florida in July or August for a month."

"I reckon they don't know how hot it gets," Polly said, shaking her head. "I'd sooner spend the summer in Hades than in Silver Beach."

"That's their problem, not mine." Wilma consulted the list of abbreviations, although by this time she'd memorized most of them. "No air conditioning, but a washer and dryer, modern kitchen with dishwasher and microwave, garden, domestic help, and a quiet neighborhood. They want to exchange cars, too. I do believe I'll write them first."

"What does George think about this?"

Wilma carefully copied the name and address, then closed the catalog and gave Polly a beady look. "Not that it's any of your business, but I haven't discussed it with him. I don't see any reason to do it until I've reached an agreement and found out exactly how much the airfare will be."

Polly decided it was too risky to ask about the finances of this crazy scheme. "Let me see your ad."

Wilma flipped open the catalog and pointed to the appropriate box. While Polly tried to make sense of the abbreviations, she sat back and dreamily imagined herself in a lush garden, sipping tea and enjoying a cool, British breeze.

Polly looked up in bewilderment. "According to what this says, the nearest airport is Orlando. Isn't Miami a sight closer?"

"The main reason people with children come to Florida is to go to Disneyworld. I want them to think it's convenient."

"Oh," Polly murmured. She consulted the list several more times. "This says you have four bedrooms and two bathrooms, Wilma. I haven't been out in your back yard lately, but last time I was there I didn't notice any swimming pool or deck with a barbecue grill. We ain't on the beach, either. The nearest one is a half-hour's drive and it's been closed for two years because of the pollution. It takes a good two hours to get to an open beach."

"The couch in the living room makes into a bed, so they can consider it a bedroom. One bathroom's plenty. I'll be the one paying the water bill at the end of the month, after all."

"Your air conditioner doesn't work any more than mine, and if you've got a microwave and a clothes dryer, you sure hide 'em well. I suppose there's golf and skiing and playgrounds and scuba diving and boating and hiking, but not anywhere around these parts. You got one thing right, though. It's a quiet neighborhood now that everyone's afraid to set foot outside because of those hoodlums. Mr. Hodkins heard gunfire just the other night."

Wilma did not respond, having returned to her fantasy. It was now replete with crumpets.

122 Palmetto Road
Silver Beach, FL 34101

Dear Sandra,

I received your letter this morning and I don't want to waste a single minute in responding. You and your husband sound like a charming couple. I shall always treasure the photograph of you and your three beautiful children. I was particularly taken with little Dorothy's dimples and angelic smile.

As I mentioned in my earlier letter, you will find our home quite comfortable and adequate for your needs. Our car is somewhat older than yours, but it will get you to Disneyworld in no time at all.

You have voiced concern about your children and the swimming pool, but you need not worry. The ad was set incorrectly. The pool is a block away at our neighborhood clubhouse. There is no lifeguard, however.

I fully intended to enclose photographs of ourselves and our house, but my husband forgot to pick up the prints at the drug store on his way home from the golf course. I'll do my best to remember to put them in the next letter.

I believe we'll follow your advice and take the train from Gatwick to Cobbet. Train travel is much more

Joan Hess

limited here, so we will leave our car at the Orlando airport for your convenience.

In the meantime, start stocking up on suntan oil for your wonderful days on the beach. I wouldn't want Dorothy's dimples to turn red.

Your dear friend in Florida,
Wilma

"Have you told George?" Polly whispered, glancing at the doorway. Noises from the television set indicated that basketball had been replaced with baseball, although it was impossible to determine if George had noticed. His only concession to the blistering resurgence of summer was a pair of stained plaid shorts.

Wilma snorted. "Yes, Polly, I have told George. Did you think I crept into the living room and took his passport photographs without him noticing?"

"Is he excited?"

"He will be when the time comes," she said firmly. "In any case, it really doesn't matter. The Millingfords are coming on the first of July whether he likes it or not. I find it hard to imagine he would enjoy sharing this house with three snotty-nosed children. Look at the photograph if you don't believe me. They look like gargoyles, especially the baby. The two older ones have the same squinty eyes as their father."

"The house looks nice."

"It does, doesn't it? If it's half as decent as that insufferably smug woman claims, we should be comfortable. The flowerbeds are pretentious, but I'm not surprised. She made a point of mentioning that they have a gardener twice a week. I was tempted to write back and say ours comes three times a week, but I let it go." She tapped the photograph. "Look at that structure near the garden wall. It's a hutch, of all things. It seems that Lucinda and Charles keep pet rabbits. Because little Dorothy has asthma and all kinds of allergies, the rabbits are not allowed in the house. The idea of stepping on a dropping makes my stomach turn."

"Will that cause a problem with Popsie?"

Wilma leaned down to stroke Popsie's satiny ears. He'd been lured away from the toilet with chocolate-chip cookies, and now crumb-flecked droplets of saliva were sprinkled beneath the table. She felt a prick of remorse at the idea of leaving him for a month, but it couldn't be helped, not if she was to have a vacation that would outshine Jewel Jacoby's. "I haven't mentioned Popsie in my letters. The boarding kennel wants twenty-five dollars a day. I've had to set aside every penny for our airfare, which is why the washing machine is still leaking. The tires on the car are bald and the engine makes such a terrible rattle that I literally hold my breath every time I drive to the store. There's absolutely no way I can get anything repaired until we build up some cash in the fall. Besides that, my Popsie is very delicate and would be miserable in a strange place. If there are any disruptions in his schedule, he begins piddling on the floor and passing wind." She looked thoughtfully at Polly and decided not to even hint that Popsie would enjoy a lengthy visit in his neighbor's home. Not after what Popsie had done to Polly's cat.

"I do want to ask a small favor of you," she continued with a conspiratorial wink. "I'm worried about the children damaging the house. I'm going to lock away all the good dinnerware, but they're quite capable of leaving muddy footprints all over the furniture and handprints on the walls. I'm hoping you'll drop by at least once a day. Just ask if they're having a pleasant vacation or something."

Polly flinched. "Won't they think I'm spying on them?"

"That's exactly what I want them to think. They need to be reminded they're guests in my home."

"Is there anything else?"

"One other favor. I'm going to leave a note in the car for them to come by your house to pick up the house key and letter regarding their stay. If you don't mind, of course?"

As dim as she was, Polly suspected the British family might be disgruntled by the time they arrived in Silver Beach. However, nothing interesting had taken place since the knifing by the clubhouse several weeks ago. Shrugging, she said, "I'll make a point of being here when they arrive."

Dear Sandra,

Welcome to Florida! I'm writing this while we pack, but I'll try very hard not to forget anything. I hope you and the family enjoyed the flight to Orlando. I was a tiny bit muddled about the distance from the airport to the house, but George insisted that it was no more than an hour's drive. How embarrassing to have discovered only the other day that it's nearly three times that far! In any case, I shall assume my map and directions were clear and you successfully arrived at my dear friend Polly Simps's house. She is excited about your visit, and will come by often to check on you.

I must apologize for the air conditioner. The repairman has assured me that the part will arrive within a matter of days and he will be there to put it in working order. Please be very careful with the washing machine. Last night I received a nasty shock that flung me across the room and left my body throbbing most painfully. I was almost convinced my heart had received enough of a jolt to kill me! You might prefer to use the launderette in town. I had a similar experience with the dishwasher—why do these things go haywire on such short notice???

I am so sorry to tell you that our cleaning woman was diagnosed with terminal liver cancer three days ago. She immediately left to spend her last few weeks with her family in Atlanta. Her son, who works as our gardener, went with her. I was so stricken that all I could do was offer her a generous sum and wish them both the best. The lawn mower is in the carport storage area. It's balky, but will start with encouragement. You can buy gas (or petrol, as you say) for it at any service station.

And now I must mention dearest Popsie, whom you've surely discovered by now. We've had him for twelve years and he's become as beloved to us as a child. I had a long and unpleasant conversation with the brutes at the boarding kennel. They made it clear that Popsie would be treated with nothing short of cruelty. He is much too delicate to withstand such abuse and estrangement from his familiar surroundings. You will find him to be only the most minor nuisance, and I implore you to behave like decent Christians and treat him with kindness.

He must be taken for a walk (in order to do his duty) three times a day, at eight in the morning, noon, and five in the afternoon. His feeding instructions, along with those for the vitamin and mineral supplements and details regarding his eye drops and insulin shots, are taped on the refrigerator. Once he becomes accustomed to the children, he will stop snapping and allow them to enter the bathroom. Until he does so, I strongly suggest that he be approached with caution. I should feel dreadful if dear little Dorothy's rosy cheeks were savaged.

The Silverado Community Beach is closed because of an overflow from a sewage disposal facility. You'll find

Miami Beach, although a bit farther, to be lovely. The presence of a lifeguard should be reassuring in that you've obviously neglected to teach your children how to swim. You might consider lessons in the future.

The refrigerator has been emptied for your convenience. I left bread and eggs for your first night's supper. Milk would have spoiled, but you'll find a packet of powdered lemonade mix for the children. Polly will give you directions to the supermarket.

The car started making a curious clanking sound only yesterday. I would have taken it to the garage had time permitted, but it was impossible to schedule an appointment. George suspects a problem with the transmission. I will leave the telephone numbers of several towing services should you experience any problems. All of them accept credit cards.

But above all, make yourselves at home!

Wilma

Ferncliffe House
Willow Springs Lane
Cobbet, Lincs LN2 3AB

15 July (as they say)

Dear Polly,

We're having an absolutely wonderful time. The house is much nicer than I expected. Everything works properly, and even the children's rooms were left tidy.

I spend a great deal of time in the garden with a cup of tea and a novel, while George pops over to the pub to shoot billiards and play darts with his cronies. Last

Sunday our lovely neighbors invited us to a picnic at the local cricket field. The game itself is incredibly stupid, but I suffered through it for the sake of cucumber sandwiches and cakes with clotted cream and jam.

I must say things are primitive. The washing machine is so small that our cleaning woman has to run it continually all three mornings every week when she's here. Her accent is droll, to put it kindly, and she is forever fixing us mysterious yet tasty casseroles. If I knew what was in them, I doubt I could choke down a single bite. The village shops are pathetically small, poorly stocked, and close at odd hours of the day. I don't know how these people have survived without a decent supermarket. And as for their spelling, you'd think the whole population was illiterate. I wonder if I'm the first person who's mentioned that they drive on the wrong side of the road.

I had reservations about the lack of air conditioning, but the days are mild and the nights cool. Sandra "conveniently" forgot to mention how often it rains; I suppose she was willing to lie simply to trick us into the exchange. She was certainly less than honest about the train ride from London. It takes a good seventy minutes.

I've searched every drawer and closet in the entire house and have yet to find a Bible. It does make one wonder what kind of people they really are. In the note I left, I begged them to treat Popsie with a Christian attitude, but now I wonder if they're even familiar with the term. Everyone is so backward in this country. For all I know, the Millingfords are Catholics—or Druids!

I must stop now. Tonight we're being treated to dinner at a local restaurant, where I shall become queasy just reading the menu. And I'm dreading tomorrow morning. Someone failed to shut the door of the hutch and the rabbits have escaped. No doubt the gardener will be upset in his amusing guttural way, since they were his responsibility. I honestly think it's for the best. The animals are filthy and one of them scratched my arm so viciously that I can still see a mark. What kind of parents would allow their children to have pets like those? Dogs are so much cleaner and more intelligent. I do believe I shall leave a note to that effect for Sandra to read when the family returns home.

Wilma

Polly was waiting on her porch when George and Wilma pulled into the driveway. She would have preferred to cower inside her house, blinds drawn and doors locked, but she knew this would only add to Wilma's impending fury. "Welcome home," she called bravely.

Wilma told George to unload the luggage, then crossed into the adjoining yard. "I feel like we've been traveling for days and days. It would have been so much easier to fly into the Miami airport, but the Millingfords had to go to Disneyworld, didn't they?"

"And they did," Polly began, then faltered as the words seemed to stick in her mouth like cotton balls (or, perhaps, clumps of rabbit fur similar to the ones the gardener had found in the meadow behind Ferncliffe House).

"So what?"

"They left two weeks ago."

"Just what are you saying, Polly Simps? I'm exhausted from the trip, and I have no desire to stand here while you make cryptic remarks about these whiny people. I'm not the least bit interested at the moment, although I suppose in a day or two when I'm rested you can tell me about them." She looked back at George, who was struggling toward the house with suitcases. "Be careful! I have several jars of jam in that bag."

Florida was still flat, so Polly's desperate desire to disappear into a gaping hole in the yard was foiled. "I think you'd better listen to me, Wilma. There were . . . some problems."

"I'm beginning to feel faint. If there's something you need to say, spit it out so I can go into my own home and give Popsie the very expensive milk biscuits I bought for him in England."

"Come inside and I'll fix you a glass of iced tea."

Wilma's nostrils flared as if she were a winded racehorse. "All I can say is this had better be good," she muttered as she followed her neighbor across the porch and through the living room. "Did the Millingfords snivel about everything? Are you going to present me with a list of all their petty complaints?"

"They didn't complain," Polly said as she put glasses on the table. "They were a little disappointed when they arrived, I think. Five minutes after I'd given them the key and your letter, Sandra came back to ask if it was indeed the right house. I said it was. Later that afternoon David came over and asked if I could take him to the grocery store, since your car wouldn't start."

"What colossal nerve! Did he think you were the local taxi service?"

Polly shrugged. "I told him I didn't have one, but I arranged for him to borrow Mr. Hodkins's car for an hour. The next morning a tow truck came for the car, and within a week or so it was repaired. During that time, they stayed inside the house for the most part. At one point the two older children came to ask me about the swimming pool, but that was the last time any of them knocked on my door."

"I'd like to think they were brought up not to pester people all the time. But as I hinted in my letter to you, they seem to be growing up in a heathen environment. You did go over there every day, didn't you?"

"I tried, Wilma, but I finally stopped. I'd ring the bell and ask how they were enjoying their visit, but whichever parent opened the door just stared at me and then closed the door without saying a word. Once I heard the baby wailing in one of the bedrooms, but other than that it was so quiet over there that I wondered what on earth they were doing."

Wilma entertained images of primitive rituals, embellishing them with her limited knowledge of Druids and gleanings from Errol Flynn movies. "Poor Popsie," she said at last. "How hideous for him. Did they walk him three times a day?"

"For a few days. Then the baby had an asthma attack and had to be taken to the hospital in an ambulance. After that, they left Popsie in the backyard, where he howled all night. The misery in that dog's voice was almost more than I could bear."

"Those barbarians! I'm going to write a letter to Mrs. Snooty Millingford and remind her that she was supposed to treat poor Popsie in a civilized, if not Christian, fashion. Your instincts were right, Polly. It's very dangerous to allow foreigners in your home."

"There's more. Once they got the car back, they took some day trips, but then two weeks ago they upped and left. It must have been late at night, because I never saw them loading the car and I made sure I kept an eye on them from my bedroom window during the day. Anyway, the key was in my mailbox one morning. I rushed over, but their luggage was gone. Everything was nice and neat, and they put a letter addressed to you on the kitchen counter."

Wilma started to comment on the unreliability of foreigners, then realized Polly was so nervous that her eyelid was twitching and her chin trembling. "What about Popsie?" she asked shrewdly, if also anxiously.

"Gone."

"Gone? What do you mean?"

"I organized a search party and we hunted for him for three days straight. I put an ad in that shopping circular and called the dog pound so many times that they promised they'd call me if they picked him up."

Wilma clasped the edge of the table and bared her teeth in a comical (at least from Polly's perspective) parody of a wild beast. "They must have stolen Popsie! What did the police say? You did call the police, didn't you? All they'd have to do is stop the car and drag those wicked Millingfords off to jail."

"They wouldn't have taken him, Wilma. When the ambulance men came to the house, I heard the father say that the baby's asthma attack was brought on by dog hairs. The last thing they'd do is put Popsie right there in the car with them and risk another attack."

"Well, I'm calling the police now," Wilma snarled as she shoved back her chair and started for the front door. "And you can forget about your jar of jam, Polly Simps. I asked you to do one little favor for me. Look what I get in return!"

George was sound asleep on the recliner as she marched through the living room, intent on the telephone in the kitchen. Of course it was too late for the police to take action. The Millingfords had safely escaped across the Atlantic Ocean, where they could ignore official demands concerning Popsie's disappearance. She could imagine the smugness on Sandra's face and her syrupy avowals of innocence. Perhaps she would feel differently when her children discovered the empty hutch.

The envelope was on the counter. Wilma ripped it open, and with an unsteady hand, took out the letter.

Dear Mrs. Chadley,

Thank you so very much for making your home available to us this last fortnight. It was not precisely what we'd anticipated, but after a bit we accepted your invitation to "make ourselves at home."

Tucked under the telephone you will find invoices from the towing service, auto repair shop, and tire shop. They were all quite gracious about awaiting your payment. The chap from the air conditioner service never came. My husband called all shops listed in the back pages of the telephone directory, but none seemed to have been the one with which you trade. He tried to have a look at it himself, but became leery that he inadvertently might damage some of the rustier parts.

After he checked the wiring, I had a go at the washing machine, but I must have done something improperly because water gushed everywhere. It made for quite a mopping.

We've changed our plans and have decided to spend the remaining fortnight touring the northern part of the state. Lucinda and Charles are frightfully keen about space technology and are exceedingly eager to visit the Kennedy Center. Dorothy adores building sand castles on the beach. Also, this will make it easier for us to leave your car at the Orlando airport as we'd arranged.

I hope you enjoyed your stay in Cobbet. Our neighbors are quite friendly in an unobtrusive way, and several of them promised to entertain you. I also hope you enjoyed Mrs. Bitney's cooking. She is such a treasure.

In honour of your return, I adapted one of Mrs.

Bitney's family recipes for steak and kidney pie. It's in the freezer in an oblong pan. When you and your husband eat it, I do so hope you'll remember our exchange.

Yours truly,
Sandra Millingford

Wilma numbly put down the letter and went to the back door. Popsie's water and food bowls were aligned neatly in one corner of the patio. A gnawed rubber ball lay in the grass. The three pages of instructions were no longer taped to the door of the refrigerator, but several cans of dog food were lined up beside the toaster.

She went into the bathroom and peered behind the toilet as if Popsie had been hiding there all this time, too wily to show himself to Polly while he awaited their return. Not so much as a hair marred the vinyl.

At last, when she could no longer avoid it, she returned to the kitchen and sat down. As her eyes were drawn toward the door of the freezer, they began to fill with tears.

Sandra Millingford had made herself at home. What else had she made?

All That Glitters

Welcome to the home of Remmington Boles and his mother, Audrey Antoinette (née Tattlinger) Boles. It is a small yet gracious house in the center of the historic district. At one time it was the site of fancy luncheons and elegant dinner parties. There have been no parties of any significance since the timely and unremarkable demise of Ralph Edward Boles. I believe this was in 1962, but it may have been the following year.

Remmington, who is called Remmie by his mother and few remaining relatives, is forty-one years old, reasonably tall, reasonably attractive. There is little else to say about his physical presence. It's likely you would trust him on first sight. He has never been unkind to animals or children.

Audrey is of an age that falls between sixty and seventy. She was once attractive in an antebellum sort of way. In her heyday thirty years ago, she was president of the Junior League and almost single-handedly raised the money for a children's cancer wing at the regional hospital.

At this moment, Audrey is in her bedroom at the top of the stairs. Although we cannot see her, we can deduce from her vaguely querulous tone that she is no longer in robust health.

"Remmie? Do you have time to find my slippers before

you leave? It seems so damp and chilly this morning. I hope there's nothing wrong with the furnace."

Her son's voice is patient and, for the most part, imbued with affection. He is not a candidate for sainthood, but he is a good son.

"There's nothing wrong with the furnace," he says as he comes into her bedroom. "Let me raise the blinds so you can enjoy the sunshine."

He takes two steps, then pauses as he does every morning. The micro-drama has been performed for many years. Very rarely does anything happen to disrupt it, and there is nothing in the air to lead Remmie to suspect this day will be extraordinary.

"No, leave them down. I can't tolerate the glare. Oh, Remmie, I pray every night that you'll never face the specter of blindness. It's so very frightening."

Two steps to her side; two squeezes of her hand. "Now, Mother, Dr. Whitbread found no symptoms of retinopathy, and he said you shouldn't worry. The ophthalmologist said the same thing only a few months ago."

Her eyes are bleached and rimmed with red, but they regard him with birdlike acuity. "You're so good to me. I don't know how I could ever get along without you."

"I'm late for work, Mother. Here are your slippers right beside the bed. I'll be home at noon to fix your lunch." He bends down to kiss her forehead, then waits to be dismissed.

"Bless you, Remmie."

Remmie Boles goes downstairs to the kitchen, rinses out his coffee cup, and props it in the rack, then makes sure his mother's tray is ready for her midmorning snack; tea bag, porcelain cup and saucer, two sugar cookies in a cellophane bag. The teapot, filled with a precise quantity of water, is on the back burner.

He enjoys the six-block walk to Boles Discount Furniture Warehouse, and produces a smile for his secretary, who is filing her fingernails. She is not overly bright, but she is very dependable—a trait much valued in small business concerns.

"Good morning, Ailene," Remmie says, collecting the mail from the corner of her desk.

"Some guy from your church called, Mr. Boles. He wants to know if you're gonna be on the bowling team this year. He says they'll take you back as long as you promise not to quit in the middle of the season like you did last year." Having been an employee for ten years, she feels entitled to make unseemly comments. "You really should get out and meet people. You're not all that old, you know, and kinda cute. There are a lot of women who'd jump at the chance to go out with a guy like you."

"Please bring me the sales tax figures from the last quarter." Remmie goes into his office and closes the door before he allows himself to react.

Ailene has made a point. Remmie is not a recluse. He has dated over the year, albeit infrequently and for no great duration. Alas, he has not been out since the fiasco that was responsible for his abandonment of the First Methodist Holy Rollers in midseason.

Yes, even Methodists can evince a sense of humor.

Lucinda was (and still is, as far as I know) a waitress at the bowling alley. He'd been dazzled by her bright red hair, mischievous grin, and body that rippled like a field of ripe wheat when she walked. She agreed to go out for drinks. One thing had led to another, first in the front seat of his car, then on the waterbed in her apartment.

The very idea of experiencing such sexual bliss every night left Remmie giddy, and he found himself pondering marriage. After a series of increasingly erotic encounters, he invited Lucinda to meet his mother.

It was a ghastly idea. Lucinda arrived in a tight purple dress that scarcely covered the tops of her thighs, and brought a bottle of whiskey as a present. In the harsh light of his living room, he could see the bags under her eyes and the slackness of her jowls. Her voice was coarse, her laugh a bray, her ripple nothing more than a cheap, seductive wiggle. He quit the bowling team immediately.

Back to work, Remmie.

He ignores the message and settles down with the figures. At eleven, he goes out to the showroom to make sure his salesmen aren't gossiping in the break room. He is heading for the counter when a woman comes through the main door and halts, her expression wary, as if she's worried that ravenous beasts are lurking under oak veneer tables and behind plaid recliners.

If Ailene hadn't made her presumptuous comments, perhaps Remmie would not have given this particular customer more than a cursory assessment. As it is, he notices she's a tiny bit plump, several inches shorter than he, and of a similar age. Her hair, short and curly, is the color of milk chocolate. She is wearing a dark skirt and white blouse, and carrying a shiny black handbag.

"May I help you?" he says.

"I'm just looking. It's hard to know where to start, isn't it?"

"Are you in the market for living room furniture? We have a good assortment on sale right now."

"I need all sorts of things, but I don't have much of a budget," she says rather sadly. "Then again, I don't have much of a house."

To his horror, her eyes fill with tears.

Remmie persuades her to accept a cup of coffee in his office, and within a half hour, possesses her story. Crystal Ambler grew up on the seedy side of the city, attended the junior college, and is now the office manager of a small medical clinic. A childless marriage ended in divorce more than five years ago. She spends her free time reading, gardening, and occasionally playing bridge with her parents and sister. She once had a cat; but it ran away and now she lives alone.

"Not very exciting, is it?" she says with a self-deprecatory laugh. "It's hard being single these days, and almost impossible to meet someone who isn't burdened with a psychosis and an outstanding warrant or two."

"Mr. Boles," Ailene says from the doorway, "your mother called to remind you to pick up syringes on your way home for lunch."

"Is your mother ill?" asks Crystal with appropriate sympathy.

"She was diagnosed with diabetes the year I graduated from college. It's manageable with daily insulin injections and a strict diet."

"It must be awfully hard on you and your wife," she begins, then gasps and rises unsteadily. "I'm sorry. It's none of my business and I shouldn't have—"

"It's perfectly all right." Remmie catches her hands between his and studies her contrite expression, spotting for the first time a little dimple on her chin. "I should be the one to apologize. You came here to look for furniture, and I've wasted your time with my questions. I do hope you'll allow me to help you find a bargain."

Crystal is amenable.

Remmie smiles thoughtfully as he walks home for lunch. There is something charmingly quaint about Miss Ambler.

She is by no means a hapless maiden awaiting rescue by a knight; when she selected the sofa, she did so with no hint of indecision or tacit plea for his approval. But at the same time, she is soft-spoken and modest. He's certain she would never wear a tight purple dress or drink whiskey. He doubts she drinks anything more potent than white wine.

He's halfway across the living room when he realizes something is acutely wrong. His mother never fails to call his name when he enters the house. It is an inviolate part of their script.

"Mother?" he calls as he hurries upstairs to her bedroom. The room is dim; the television, invariably set on a game show, is silent. The figure on the bed is motionless. "Mother?" he repeats with a growing sense of panic.

"Remmie, thank God you're here. I feel so weak. I tried to call you, but I couldn't even lift the receiver."

"Shall I call for an ambulance?"

"No, I simply need something to nibble on to elevate my blood sugar. If it's not too much trouble, would you please bring the cookies from this morning?"

"You skipped your snack? Dr. Whitbread stressed how very vital it is that you stay on your schedule. Maybe I should call him."

"All I need are the cookies, Remmie." Despite her avowed weakness, she picks up the clock and squints at it. "My goodness, you're almost an hour late. Was there an emergency at the store?"

"A minor one," he murmurs.

Remmie calls Crystal that evening to make sure she is pleased with her selection. She shyly invites him to come by some time and see how well the sofa goes with the drapes. Remmie professes eagerness to do so, and suggests Saturday morning. Although Crystal sounds disappointed, she promises coffee and cake.

The week progresses uneventfully. Whatever has caused Audrey's bout of weakness has not recurred, although she has noticed a disturbing new symptom and broaches it after the evening news is over.

She holds out a hand. "Feel my fingers, Remmie. They're so swollen I haven't been able to wear any of my rings. Perhaps you should take all my jewelry down to the bank tomorrow morning and put it in the safe-deposit box. If it's not too much bother, of course. It's so maddening not to be able to do things for myself. I know I'm such a terrible burden on you."

"I'll do it Saturday morning," Remmie says. "I have some other errands, and I'll be in that neighborhood."

"Errands? I hate to think of you spending your weekend driving all over town instead of having a chance to relax around the house. You work so hard all week."

"I enjoy getting out." He picks up her tray and heads for the kitchen.

Saturday.

Remmie grimaces as he pulls into the driveway. His mother's jewelry is still in the glove compartment, and the bank closes at noon on Saturdays. His mother will spend the weekend fretting if she finds out about his negligence, but there's no reason why she will. A good son does not cause his mother unnecessary concern.

He sits in the car and replays his visit. Upon opening the door, Crystal hadn't thrown herself into his arms, but she'd held his hand several seconds longer than decorum dictates. Their conversation had been lively. They'd parted with yet another warm handshake.

He locks the glove compartment and goes inside. And freezes as he sees his mother slumped on the sofa, her hands splayed across her chest and her eyes closed.

"Mother!" he says as he sinks to her side. "Can you hear me?"

"I'm conscious," Audrey says dully. "I was on my way to the kitchen when I felt so dizzy I almost fell."

"Let me help you back to bed, and then I'll call the doctor." Remmie picks her up and carries her to her bedroom, settles her on the bed, and reaches for the telephone.

"No, don't disturb Dr. Whitbread. He's entitled to his weekends, just as you are. If I'm not better on Monday, you can call him then."

"Are you sure?" asks Remmie, alarmed at the thinness of her voice.

"It's very dear of you to be so concerned about me, Remmie. Most children put their ailing parents in nursing homes and try to forget about them. The poor old things lose what wits they have and spend their last days drooling and being tormented by sadistic nurses."

"This is your home, Mother. Why don't you take a little nap while I fix your lunch?"

"Bless you," she says with a sigh. He's almost to the door when she adds, "There was a call for you half an hour ago. A woman with a trailer park sort of name said you'd left your gloves at her house. I tried to catch you at the bank to relay the message, but they said you hadn't come in. I hope they weren't your suede gloves, Remmie. I ordered them from Italy, you know."

"I know." He urges himself back into motion. Had he subconsciously chosen to leave his gloves at Crystal's house so he'd have another excuse to call her? He ponders the possibility as he washes lettuce and slices a tomato.

★ ★ ★ ★ ★

Audrey is strangely quiet all afternoon and declines his offer to play gin rummy after dinner. Remmie finally breaks down and tells her about Crystal Ambler.

"She sounds very nice," says Audrey. "She lives in that neighborhood beyond the interstate, you said? Your father and I made a point of never driving through that area after dark, even if it meant going miles out of our way." She pauses as if reliving a long and torturous detour, then says, "What exactly does this woman do?"

Audrey listens as Remmie describes Crystal's job, her clean, if somewhat Spartan, house, her garden, even her new sofa. "She sounds very nice," is all she says as she limps across the dining room and down the hall. "Very nice."

Sunday, Sunday.

Remmie calls Crystal while his mother is napping. After he apologizes for leaving his gloves, he invites her to meet him after work on Monday for a glass of wine.

Monday.

Remmie tells his mother he'll be working late in preparation for the inventory-reduction sale. He uses the same excuse when he takes Crystal to dinner later that week. On Saturday afternoon, he makes an ambiguous reference to the hardware store and takes Crystal for a drive in the country. Afterward, he feels foolish when Audrey not only brings up Crystal's name, but encourages him to ask her out. He admits they have plans.

"Dinner on Wednesday?" murmurs Audrey, carefully folding her napkin and placing it on the table. "What a lovely idea, Remmie. I'm sure she'll be thrilled to have a meal in a proper restaurant."

"Would you like me to see if Miss McCloud can sit with you while I'm out?"

"I wouldn't dream of bothering her. After all, I'm here by myself every day. I'm so used to being alone that I'll scarcely notice that you're out with this woman."

"I'd like to meet your mother," Crystal says as they dally over coffee in her living room. "You're obviously devoted to her."

"My father left a very small estate. My mother insisted on working at a clothing shop to put me through college, then used the last of the insurance money to finance the store. Before her illness grew more debilitating, she came down to the showroom at night and dusted the displays." Remmie smiles gently. "I'd like you to meet her. She's asked me all about you, and I think she's beginning to suspect I might be . . ."

"Be what?"

"Falling in love," he says, then leans forward and kisses her. When she responds, he slides his arm behind her back and marvels at the supple contours. Their kisses intensify, as do Remmie's caresses and her tiny moans. His hand finds its way beneath her sweater to her round breasts. His mind swirls with deliciously impure images.

Therefore, he's startled when she pulls back and moves to the far end of the sofa. For an alarming moment, she looks close to tears, but she takes a shuddery breath and says, "No, Remmie, I'm not going to have an affair. I shouldn't have gone out with you in the first place. I'm too old to get into another pointless relationship. I'd rather get a cat."

Remmie bites back a groan. "Crystal, darling, I'd never do anything to hurt you. I don't want a pointless relationship, either."

"Then take me home to meet your mother."

He frowns at the obstinate edge in her voice. "I will when the time's right. Mother's been fretting about her blood pressure lately, and I don't want to excite her more than necessary."

"Maybe you'd better go home and check on her," Crystal says as she stands up. However, rather than hurrying him out the door, she presses her body against his and kisses him with such fierce passion that he nearly loses his balance. "There'll be more of this when we're engaged," she promises in a warm, moist whisper. She goes on to describe what lies in store after they're married.

The constraints of the genre prevent me from providing details.

Time Flies.

"Does your friend drive an old white Honda?" Audrey asks Remmie while he's massaging her feet to stimulate circulation.

He gives her a surprised look. "Why do you ask?"

"Someone who matches the description has driven by here several times. It most likely wasn't her, though. This woman had the predatory gleam of a real estate appraiser trying to decide how much our house is worth." Audrey manages a weak chuckle. "And of course I can barely see the street from my window these days. It's all a matter of time before I'm no longer a burden, Remmie, and you'll be free to get on with your life."

"Don't say that, Mother," he says as he strokes her wispy gray hair. A sudden vision of the future floods his mind: his mother's bedroom is unlit and empty, but farther down the hall, Crystal smiles from his bed, her arms outstretched and her breasts heaving beneath a silky black gown.

He realizes his mother is staring at him and wipes a sheen of perspiration off his forehead. "Don't say that," he repeats.

★ ★ ★ ★ ★

Several more weeks pass, and then back to Boles Discount Furniture Warehouse we go.

This morning Ailene is typing slowly but steadily. "Crystal called," she says without looking up. "She said to tell you that she can't go to the movies tonight."

"Did she say why?"

"Something about baby-sitting for her sister. Oh, and your mother called right before you got here. She wants you to pick up some ointment for her blisters. She said you'd know what kind and where to get it."

Remmie closes his office door, reaches for the telephone, and then lowers his hand. Crystal has made it clear that he's not to call her at the clinic. But this is the second time this week she's canceled their date to do a favor for her sister. Last week she met him at the door and announced she was going out with some friends from the clinic. Remmie had not been invited to join them.

Can he be losing her? When they're together on the sofa, her passion seems to rival his own. Although she continues to refuse to make love, she has found ways to soften his frustration. She swears she has never loved anyone as deeply.

He collapses in his chair, cradles his head in his hands, and silently mouths her name.

When Remmie comes into the living room, he is shocked. He is stunned, bewildered, and profoundly inarticulate. The one thing he is not prepared to see is his mother sitting at one end of the sofa and Crystal at the other. A tray with teacups and saucers resides on the coffee table, a few crumbs indicative that cookies have been consumed.

"Crystal," he gasps.

"Remmie, dear," his mother says chidingly, "that's no way

101

to welcome a guest into our home. Have you forgotten your manners?"

Crystal's smile is as sweet as the sugar granules on the tray. "I was in the neighborhood, and it seemed like time to stop by and meet your mother. We've been having a lovely chat."

"Oh, yes," says Audrey. "A lovely chat."

Remmie sinks down on the edge of the recliner, aware his mouth is slack. "That's good," he says at last.

Audrey nods. "Crystal and I discovered a most amazing coincidence. It seems her mother used to clean house for Laetitia Whimsey, who was in my garden club for years."

"Amazing," Remmie says, glaring at Crystal. He's angry at her effrontery in coming, but she refuses to acknowledge him and listens attentively as Audrey reminisces about her garden club.

Out on the porch, however, Crystal crosses her arms and gazes defiantly at him. "This meeting was long overdue," she says, "and you've been stalling. Well, now I've met her. She seems to like me well enough, and I'm sure we'll get along just fine in the future. We do have a future, don't we?"

"Of course we do," he says, shocked by her vehemence. "I was only waiting until Mother . . ."

"Dies?"

Remmie steps back and clutches the rail. "Don't be ridiculous. She's experiencing numbness in her lower legs and feet, and the doctor recommended tests for arteriosclerosis. Mother is always distraught about going into the hospital."

"And then what, Remmie? Will she have problems with her kidneys? Will her blood pressure fluctuate?"

"I don't know, Crystal. Her condition is very delicate, but the doctor seems to feel that in general her prognosis is good."

"Then what's the delay?" she counters. "I believed you when you told me that you love me. Otherwise, I would have broken off our relationship long before I became emotionally involved. There are plenty of women who'll sleep with you, Remmie—if that's all you want."

He stares as she marches down the steps and across the street to her little white car. He remains on the porch even after she has driven away without so much as a glance in his direction.

"Remmie?" calls his mother. "Could you be a dear and help me upstairs? I wasn't expecting any visitors, and now I'm exhausted. There's no rush, of course. I'll just sit here in the dark until you have a moment."

January proves to be the cruelest month.

Crystal allows Remmie to take her out several times, and permits him a few more liberties on the sofa, for which he is grateful. On the other hand, he senses a reticence on her part to abandon herself to his embraces. They both avoid any references to Audrey, who continues to encourage him to go out with Crystal.

Remmie begins to feel as if he's losing his mind. He's obsessed with Crystal; his waking hours are haunted by memories of how she feels in his arms. His dreams are so explicit that he awakens drenched with sweat and shivering with frustration.

The obvious question arises: Why does he not propose marriage? If he could answer this, he would. For the most part, Crystal is the girl of his dreams (if he and I may employ the cliché). She has shown a flicker of annoyance now and then, but she is quick to apologize and kiss away his injured feelings. She has joined his church. On two occasions she has brought Audrey flowers and perky greeting cards.

When Audrey mentions Crystal's name, Remmie listens intently for any nuances in her voice. He's perceptive enough to anticipate a petty display of jealousy, but thus far he has not seen it. Audrey maintains that she is fond of Crystal, that she enjoys their infrequent but pleasant conversations.

Why is he incapable of proposing?

Mercifully, January ends and we ease into February, a month fraught with significance for young and old lovers alike.

"Does Crystal have a brother?" asks Audrey one morning as Remmie is straightening her blanket.

"I don't think so."

"How odd," she says under her breath.

"Why would you think she has a brother, Mother?"

"It's so silly that I hate to confess." Audrey sighs and looks away, then adds, "I called her house yesterday morning to thank her for the romance novel she sent. A man answered the telephone, and I was so unnerved that I hung up without saying a word. It was quite early; you'd just left for work."

Remmie is aware that two days ago Crystal canceled their plans for dinner, saying that she needed to work on files from the clinic. He has not spoken to her since then, although he has left messages for her to call.

"It must have been a plumber," Audrey says dismissively. "Would you check the thermostat, dear? I can hardly wiggle my toes."

As Valentine's Day approaches, Remmie becomes more and more distracted. Crystal denies having a brother; he's too embarrassed to say anything further. He feels as if he's driving down a steep mountain road, tires skidding, brakes smoking and squealing, gravel spewing behind him.

He is staring at the calendar when Ailene comes into his office.

"Here's the candy," she says, putting down a plain white box that has come in the morning mail. "You should get a medal or something for going to all this trouble every year. It must cost twice as much as regular candy."

"It's one of our little traditions. I've told Mother she can have sugar free chocolate all year, but she says it's sweeter because it's a Valentine's Day gift."

"You doing something special with Crystal?" asks Ailene, who has been monitoring the relationship with a healthy curiosity.

Remmie comes to a decision. "Yes, I am," he says without taking his eyes off the white box.

Late in the morning, he calls Audrey and tells her that he is unable to come home to prepare her lunch, citing the need to run errands. She wishes him a profitable hour and assures him she will have a nice bowl of soup.

Remmie goes to the bank and gains access to the safe deposit box. The jewelry is in a brown felt pouch. He spreads it open and finds the diamond engagement ring given to his mother fifty-odd years ago. If he wished, he could buy a bigger and more impressive one, but he hopes Crystal will accept this as a loving tribute to his mother.

At the drugstore, he buys two heart-shaped boxes of candy. One is red, the other white, and both have glittery bows. He finds a sentimental card for his mother, who will re-read it many times before adding it to the collection in her dresser drawer.

When he returns to the office, he opens the white box and dumps the sumptuous chocolates on Ailene's desk. He then refills the box with the sugar-free chocolates made especially for diabetics, writes a loving message to his mother, and tucks the card under the pink ribbon.

Gnawing his lip, he dials the telephone number of a cozy country inn that is a hundred miles away. He makes reservations for dinner for the evening of February 14.

Despite a sudden dryness in his mouth, he also reserves a room with a fireplace and a double bed.

Crystal agrees to dinner. Remmie does not mention the room reservation. He will wait until they are sipping wine and savoring whatever decadently rich dessert the inn has prepared for the event, then slip the ring on her finger and ask her to marry him. He feels a warm tingle as he envisions what will follow.

"How romantic," murmurs Audrey as he describes the plans he has made, although he alludes only obliquely to what he hopes will transpire after his proposal. He's aware that she disapproves of sexual activity outside of wedlock, but he is over forty, after all.

He realizes he is blushing and wills himself to stop behaving like a bashful adolescent. "I'll call Miss McCloud and ask her to stay with you. That way, if you feel dizzy or need extra insulin, she'll be there to help you."

"Don't be absurd," she responds curtly.

"But I'll worry about you if you're here alone all night."

"I can take care of myself—and don't call her against my wishes. If she shows up at the front door, I'll send her away. Now please stop dithering and bring me another blanket. My feet feel as though they're frozen."

He goes to the linen closet in the hallway. As he takes a blanket from the shelf, he hears a peculiar thump. He dashes to his mother's bedroom and finds her lying on the floor like a discarded rag doll.

★ ★ ★ ★ ★

"Did she break any bones?" asks Crystal.

Remmie puts down his coffee cup and shrugs. "No, she just has some bad bruises. They kept her overnight at the hospital for observation, but Dr. Whitbread insisted she'd be more comfortable in her own bed. I took her home after I got off work."

"And left her alone?"

"Of course not," he says, appalled that she would even ask. "Miss McCloud stopped by with a plant, and I took the opportunity to come see you for a few minutes." He looks at his watch and stands up. "I'd better go."

Crystal stands up but does not move toward him. "Does this mean our Valentine dinner date is off? If you're afraid to leave your mother for more than thirty minutes, I'd like to know it right now. There's a new doctor at the clinic who's asked me out a couple of times. He's single, and he doesn't make plans around his mother."

"We're still going," he says hastily.

She goes to the door and opens it. "You'd better go home, Remmie. I hear your mother calling."

Oddly enough, Remmie almost hears her, too.

Audrey is unable to sleep because of her pain. At least once a night she calls out for Remmie, who hurries into her room with a glass of water and a white pill. Each time she apologizes at length for disturbing him.

"You know who Crystal reminds me of?" asks Audrey as Remmie pauses. He is reading the newspaper to her because her eyesight has worsened. It has become a new addition to their evening ritual.

"Who?"

"That woman from the bowling alley. They both have a certain hardness about their eyes. Not that Crystal is anything like . . . what was her name?"

"Lucinda," supplies Remmie. He zeroes in on a story concerning a charity fund-raiser and begins to read.

Too loudly, I'm afraid.

Valentine's Day.

Remmie hands his mother a notebook. Names and telephone number are written in a heavy black hand; surely she can make them out should an emergency arise. "It's not too late to call Miss McCloud, Mother. She said she will be delighted to stay with you. If you prefer, she can stay downstairs and you won't even know she's here."

"Absolutely not."

"If you're sure," he says. He has already made his decision, but it is not too late for Audrey to change the course of her destiny. He looks down at her. Her lower lip is extended and her jaw is rigid.

He realizes that when next he sees her, she will be at peace. Blinking back tears, he bends down to brush his lips across her forehead. "Good-bye, Mother," he whispers.

"Good-bye, Mrs. Boles," Crystal says from the doorway. She is holding something behind her back and scuffling her feet as if she were a small child. She gives Remmie a conspiratorial smile. "Aren't you forgetting to give your mother something?"

Remmie's face is bloodless as he takes the white heart-shaped box and presents it to Audrey. "I didn't forget," he says. "Special candy for a special person. Don't eat so much you get a tummy ache."

"Don't condescend to me," Audrey says coldly, but her expression softens as she reaches up to squeeze his hand. "I love these chocolates almost as much as I love you, Remmie. One of these days you won't have to go to all the bother to order them just for me."

Remmie stumbles as he leaves the room, brushing past Crystal as though she were nothing more substantial than a shadow.

Unamused, she follows him downstairs to the kitchen, where a second box of chocolates sits on the table. "Did you order them just for me?" she says, mimicking Audrey's simpery voice.

The trip has not started on a happy note, obviously. Remmie curses as he fights traffic until they are clear of the city, and only then does he loosen his grip on the steering wheel and glance at Crystal.

"You look nervous," he comments.

"So do you." She opens the box of chocolates and offers it to him.

He recoils, then regains control of himself. "Maybe later," he mumbles unhappily.

"Are you worried about your mother?"

"Of course I am. What if she has a dizzy spell and takes another fall? She could break her hip this time and be in such pain that she's unable to call for help."

"She'll be all right," Crystal says as she selects a chocolate and pops it in her mouth. A surprised expression crosses her face, but Remmie is in the midst of passing a truck and does not notice.

In fact, he is so distracted that he fails to respond when she comments on the scenery, and again when she cautions him to slow down as they approach a small town.

She finally taps him on the shoulder. "What's the matter with you, Remmie? Do you want to turn around and go home to check on you mother?"

Sweat dribbles down his forehead. His breathing is irregular, his lips quivering, his eyes darting, his hands once again gripping the steering wheel so tightly that his fingers are unnaturally pale.

"Remmie!" Crystal says, suddenly frightened. "What's wrong?"

He pulls to the shoulder, stops, and leans his head against the steering wheel. "I can't go through with it," he says with a whimper. "I thought I could, but I just can't do it. I'll have to find a telephone and call her before it's too late—even if it means she'll hate me for the rest of her life." He begins to cry. "How could I have betrayed her like this?"

"What are you talking about?"

"I switched the candy. The sugar will put her in a diabetic coma, and it's likely to be fatal unless she gets emergency treatment. I have to call her. If she doesn't answer, I'll call Dr. Whitbread and have him go to the house." He sits up and wipes his cheeks. "Maybe it's not too late. We've only been gone half—"

"It's not too late," Crystals snaps, "and you don't need to call anyone, especially this doctor. You'll be confessing to attempted murder. I doubt the jury will feel much sympathy."

"I don't deserve any sympathy, and I don't care what happens to me. We've got to find a telephone."

She reaches over to take the key from the ignition. After a moment of reflection, she says, "Your mother is not in danger. While I was waiting in the kitchen, I opened both boxes and figured out what you'd done. I switched them back, Remmie. Audrey is contentedly eating sugar-free chocolates."

"She is?" he says numbly.

Crystal's nod lacks enthusiasm and her smile is strained. "Yes, she sure is. I knew you couldn't live with yourself if you did something so terrible."

Remmie finally convinces himself that she is telling the truth and his mother is not in danger. "I suppose I'd better take you home."

"Why?"

"You must loathe me."

"I'll get over it," Crystal says, shrugging. "What I think we'll do is have our dinner and spend the night at this inn. Tomorrow morning we can go to the local courthouse and get a marriage license, and find a justice of the peace. Audrey will be surprised, of course, but she'll get over it more quickly if it's a done deal."

Remmie is more surprised than Audrey will ever be. "You want to get married—knowing that I tried to murder my mother? Don't you want some time to think about it?"

"I assumed you were going to propose this evening, and I'd decided to accept. I've already given my notice at the clinic so that I can stay home and take care of your mother."

Remmie attempts to decipher the odd determination in her voice, but finally gives up and leans over to kiss her. "I brought a ring to give you over dinner," he admits. "It's the one my father presented to my mother on their second date."

"How thoughtful," she says. "You really must call your mother as soon as we check in and reassure yourself that she's perfectly fine."

And so Remmie and Crystal dine by candlelight and make love under a ruffled canopy. The following morning, a license is procured and a justice of the peace conducts a brief ceremony. The witnesses find it remarkably romantic and are teary as the groom kisses the bride.

Only later, as Remmie catches sight of the white heart-shaped box on his mother's bedside table, does he ask himself the obvious question: How did Crystal know to switch back the chocolates?

He does not ask her, however. He is a good husband as well as a good son.

And there is always next year.

The Cremains of the Day

Eloise Bainbury realized it was far too early in the day for sherry, much less gin, but there she was, composed but a bit teary, wringing her hands and staring numbly at the Louis XVI armoire that had been refitted as a liquor cabinet. Her hands shook, but somehow she managed to fill the glass without splattering her wool skirt. How foolishly she was behaving, she thought with a sigh. This was not the first time he'd stayed out all night, prowling the streets and eventually sauntering home as if he'd spent the night in a church waxing the pews. She knew better.

She was standing at the kitchen window when her attorney, Milton Carruthers, called with the bad news. It came in installments, as always, and never in the trite good news–bad news format.

"I'm sorry about this, Eloise," he began nervously. "The accountant's gone over all the tax returns. He said there were some questionable deductions but nothing we can use in court. I warned you that it would be a waste of money."

"So instead of facing his responsibility to me, Justin will go on with his sumptuous lifestyle while I try to find a job in a department store or fast-food establishment? I'm fifty-seven, Milt—not twenty-seven like that tramp he intends to marry as soon as the divorce is final." Eloise took an unladylike gulp of gin, shuddered, and continued in a slightly raspier voice. "You know as well as I that Justin has stashed money in other accounts across the country. Can't you just make him tell you? What about the judge?"

"Oh, Eloise," Milt said in such a tortured voice that she could easily imagine his face screwing up like a dried apricot. "We've been over this time and again. As long as Justin denies the accounts exist and we can't prove that they do, our hands are tied. His attorney dropped off another proposal for the property settlement. It's closer to what we asked for initially, although hardly a capitulation. Why don't you schedule an appointment with my secretary for this afternoon and we'll review it?"

"I suppose so," she said without enthusiasm.

"There's something else I have to tell you. The judge signed a restraining order this morning. If you continue to harass Justin at his house or place of business, you'll be subject to contempt charges. I promise you that the amenities at the jail are not up to your standards."

Eloise sniffed. "I have no idea what you're talking about. I have never harassed Justin at any place or time since he moved out three months ago. Why, even when he was staying at the tramp's apartment, I never so much as made a crank call."

Despite her frigid tone, she was smiling at what she imagined Milt's expression to be as he floundered for a tactful response. Men, she thought, were like agitated guppies when it came to civilized discourse. "Don't you believe me?" she added.

"You had all of the girl's mail forwarded to Azerbaijan."

"Don't be absurd. I have no idea how to spell it."

Milt cleared his throat. "You sprayed Super Glue in the

locks of his car doors. You put him down as a new subscriber to one hundred and fifty-three periodicals. In his name you pledged ten thousand dollars to a televangelist whose organization is infamous for its tenacity, and the next week used his calling card number to spend seventy-six hours talking to a psychic friend."

"Nonsense," Eloise said firmly.

"Justin and his attorney were the only two people in the courtroom not sniggering, but the judge signed the order and you have to comply with it. Please, Eloise, no more jokes."

"I am the maligned party, and I deeply resent these accusations, Milton. I do hope it won't be necessary to have a word with your father."

"Only if you have a Ouija board, Eloise. He died twenty years ago." Milt made a small noise that to others might have been interpreted as frustration. Since Eloise would not condone such a reaction, she could only assume he was experiencing allergy problems. It seemed likely, since most of his conversations these days were interspersed with snuffles and grunts. They were actually rather dear, as if Milt were a beloved asthmatic hound that had won the honored position on the hearth.

Eloise did approve of loyalty. "Yes, dear. No, dear. I'll make the appointment and I won't continue doing these things I never did to begin with. We will bargain in good faith and settle this once and for all. You'll receive your very hefty fee, Justin will honeymoon with the tramp, and I will live out my days in a trailer park. Will you and Maggie miss me at the country club?"

"That's the other thing," Milt said, now sounding as if he wished he were in the outlying suburbs of Baku, which everyone knows is the capital of Azerbaijan. "Justin and Kelli were there last night. Maggie was not the only woman who had her claws out as if she were a peregrine falcon. The consensus was that he should have waited until the divorce was final, but there he was . . . with her. Trust me, Eloise, not one person in the room knew what to do except mumble and nod."

"We do what we must," murmured Eloise, wondering how next to sabotage Justin's mail now that the magazines and other periodicals had been halted. Of course, one hundred fifty-three did not begin to cover the available subscriptions when one chanced upon coupons that requested only a circle and an address. Perhaps it would be better to concentrate on other venues. After all, she'd never seriously considered the possibility of having his car reported as stolen or calling in a tip to the television show *America's Most Wanted*.

Shivers of gleeful expectancy ran down her spine as she replaced the receiver, but they subsided as she realized he still had not returned. She went to the window and pulled back the drapes. The front lawn was populated only by a robin on the impeccable grass and a mockingbird at the feeder.

He was usually home by dawn, demanding to be let in despite his ill-defined transgressions. More often than not, Eloise was obliged to daub his wounds with peroxide and judiciously apply Band-Aids to whatever bits of anatomy were oozing blood. All this solicitude was accepted without emotion, without gratitude, as if he felt it was nothing more than his just desserts for bothering to return home at all.

Puddy, Eloise thought with a flicker of irritation, could be a very naughty cat at times. But he was all she had left to keep her company. She and Justin had not been able to have children. They'd looked into adoption, but she'd always suspected he was much too self-centered to truly want a potential disruption in his life. They'd turned their energies elsewhere, he to his automobile dealership (Lincoln-Mercury) and golf game (single-digit handicap), and she to her clubs (garden and book) and charitable endeavors (historical society, hospital auxiliary, symphony guild).

And Puddy, of course. He'd arrived one rainy night, a sodden little creature, emaciated, wide-eyed with panic but desperate for food and warmth. The following morning Justin had suggested she take the kitten to the animal shelter, but Eloise was already enchanted with her foundling.

It had been seven years since Puddy had arrived—and nearly twelve hours since he'd swaggered out into the backyard and disappeared. He was wearing his collar with an engraved tag bearing her telephone number, so it did not seem likely he was lapping milk in someone else's kitchen, or even yowling in a cage at the animal shelter.

To distract herself, Eloise called Milt's secretary and arranged an appointment later in the day, then looked up the number of the local newspaper and asked to be connected to the classified advertising department.

"Here's what I want in the ad," she said to the young woman who answered. "Must sacrifice entire collection of Elvis memorabilia, including complete record set, home movies filmed inside Graceland, and an authenticated love letter, handwritten and signed, to Priscilla from Germany. Can be viewed anytime day or night. All offers will be considered, no matter how low." She gave Justin's address, then asked the woman to read it back to make sure she'd phrased it properly.

"Don't you want to give a name and a telephone number?" the woman said. "Most people do."

Eloise coughed delicately. "Our phone has been disconnected due to a financial crisis. I'm calling from a neighbor's house. Please send the bill to the address I gave you."

After she replaced the receiver, she went outside and circled the house in hopes Puddy was sleeping off his night's depravities under a hydrangea. The garden was especially magnificent this year, the envy of the entire garden club membership. A local television station had used footage of it during a tribute to springtime.

The idea of being forced to move into an apartment was more painful than Justin's announcement that he was leaving her for an uneducated, ill-bred secretary at his dealership. She'd been shocked, of course, and hurt. Her women friends had rallied around her at first, including her in luncheons and theater parties, but their collective concern was waning. Eloise knew that Justin and his tramp were being entertained on some of the same patios she had once frequented.

When she went back into the kitchen, she noticed that the red light on the coffeepot was no longer lit. The control panel of the microwave no longer showed the time. The light on the ceiling failed to blink on, as did lights in the hall and living room.

Eloise called the electric company and reported that her power was out. A weary-sounding woman asked for her address, then came back onto the line and said, "Yeah, it was cut off this morning as per customer's request. We're going to need a forwarding address for the final bill, ma'am."

"I did not make any request."

"I got your account on the screen, and it says you did last week, says you're moving as of today. Like I said, we're going to need your new address."

It took Eloise more than an hour to convince the various strata of the electric company that she had no intention of moving—or of living by candlelight. Once she'd been given a promise that her power would be restored before evening, she poured herself a second glass of gin and sat down to make posters telling of Puddy's disappearance and offering an unspecified reward.

She left the house in time to tape the posters onto telephone poles around the neighborhood, then drove to Milt's office.

Thirty minutes later she threw down the proposal. "Absolutely not!" she said, her face flushed and her jaw quivering with outrage. "I don't care about his mother's silver service and his precious antique golf clubs, but I refuse to allow the house to be sold. I've spent countless hours in the garden over the years.

"Furthermore, I cannot believe Justin earns less than fifty thousand dollars a year, Milt, and can get away with offering me alimony of one thousand dollars a month. He used to complain that he sold so many cars he could barely keep a minimal inventory. He won a company-sponsored vacation every single year, and he has enough gold plaques to pave the Yellow Brick Road."

"I know that as well as you," Milt said patiently, "but we're stuck with the figure. The accountant discovered that the vast majority of Justin's living expenses are listed as corporate expenditures. Club memberships and expensive restaurants to entertain clients. Travel to explore the feasibility of satellite dealerships. The corporation is currently paying for his house, telephones, car and health insurance—"

"Oh, stop." Eloise took a tissue from her purse and began to shred it as if it were made of Justin's flesh. When the last fragment fluttered to the floor, she picked up the proposal between her fingertips and dropped it in the trash basket beside the desk. "I refuse to sign any property settlement that deprives me of my home and fails to provide for me in the fashion to which I am accustomed. I may not be able to prevent the divorce from taking place, but I intend to delay it as long as possible. File something to that effect."

"Eloise," Milt whimpered, but it was too late. She sailed out of the office, then drove home as quickly as she dared, hoping beyond hope to find Puddy complaining in the kitchen about his litter box (which, for the record, was pristine, but Puddy could be unreasonable).

She was unable to do more than play with a bowl of soup that evening, torn as she was between Puddy's disappearance and Justin's transparent attempt at chicanery. Did thirty years of marriage mean nothing more in the eyes of the court than a cold-blooded division of whatever property Justin opted to put on the chopping block? What about her career, cut short during college? The children she'd been denied? The so-called golden years?

If only Puddy would come home, she thought as she unsuccessfully battled back tears, if only a warm, purring body were curled in her lap, offering unconditional love in exchange for the meager emotions she herself had to offer after a lifetime with Justin.

Puddy was nowhere to be found in the morning. Eloise called the animal shelter, but as she'd anticipated, no twenty-pound male cats had been nabbed on the street. Puddy would have required a battalion to take him captive. Then where was he?

For the second morning in a row, Eloise scorned tea for gin. And why not? Her lawyer disliked her, her soon-to-be ex-husband was making a pathetic attempt to coerce her into a menial existence of poverty and servitude, her friends had deserted her, and her only source of uncritical devotion had chosen to abandon her.

She passed the morning clad in plastic gloves, writing graphic death threats to various political figures, signing them with an arrogantly scrawled X, and using Justin's return address on the envelopes. She was in the middle of clipping letters from magazines that would eventually create a message that a bomb would be found in one of the local elementary schools if Kelli Kennison was not rehired as a substitute when the doorbell rang.

No one was visible when she opened the door. On the welcome mat was an envelope with no address. Doubting that Justin had discovered the technology for so thin a bomb, Eloise opened the envelope and read: "I have the cat. You know what you need to do."

Her initial reaction was instinctive but futile. Justin's driveway and, indeed, the entire street for several blocks in both directions, was jammed with pickup trucks, station wagons, and peculiar-looking people on foot, clad in sequined jackets. Many held garish guitars and were grouping to sing, as if this were a street festival.

Eloise watched them for a long while, marveling at their hair, then drove to Milt's office, barged through the reception room, and found him in conversation with a white-haired man who may or may not have been a senior partner. Eloise did not care. She slammed down the cryptic note and said, "Call the district attorney! This is nothing more than blackmail!"

The white-haired man who may or may not have been a senior partner grabbed his briefcase and scurried out of the room. Milton Carruthers, who'd just seen his best shot at a promotion evaporate, picked up the paper and read it with only a faint wuffle.

"Eloise," he said, "this isn't blackmail. It could be a message from your paperboy."

"And I could be Lisa Marie Presley Jackson," she retorted as she poked him in the chest. "I can tolerate only so much,

Milt. I stayed calm when Justin dumped me for an ignorant, flat-bellied little tramp. I said nothing when you and Maggie invited them into your home last—"

"Oh, Eloise," Milt said, clutching her hand, "I'd hoped you would understand that was business. Our firm has always had a policy of—"

"Can it. Justin can hawk my soul, trash my remaining years, hold me up to ridicule in the community, even drive me into poverty and obscurity—but he will not steal Puddy! Do you understand, Milt? He will not take away the only thing I have left on this miserable planet! He will not!" She lunged at him, her hands curled and her expression distorted with anguish. "I must have Puddy!"

Milt's secretary opened the door, then hastily closed it as Eloise sank back into the sofa that was conveniently situated to prevent clients overwhelmed with legal realities from flinging themselves out the window. A three-story dive was rarely fatal, but the firm of Guzman, Kirkpatrick, and Kirkpatrick preferred swoons to accusations of negligence.

"Do something," Eloise said in a somewhat calmer voice, although her demeanor remained suspect.

"What can I do? We can't be sure this is from Justin. It sounds as though it is, that he has the cat and is willing to use it as a bargaining ploy—but we can't prove it." Milt pushed a button on his intercom. "Marsha, please bring a cup of tea for Mrs. Bainbury."

Eloise sat up and found her purse. "I have no need of tea, Milton. I had hoped that you could do something, but I see that you can't. I shall go home now and wait for a further message."

She sailed out of his office, not so much calm as determined to do what was necessary to liberate Puddy from the evil clutches of a man she'd once respected and now loathed as if he were an emissary from hell. He and his tramp, she thought, as she drove home without regard for her personal safety or that of small children chasing balls into the street. Up until now, the pranks had been somewhat . . . well, if not harmless . . . well, not exactly heinous. She'd done nothing that wasn't deserved. After all, it had been her life that was snatched from under her feet like a frayed area rug, sending her head over heels, depriving her of the essence of her existence.

Eloise was exhausted the next morning, having been unable to sleep for even the briefest amount of time. The house was too quiet without Puddy's repertoire of yowls and rumbles of contentment. No accusatory eyes watched her as she came into the kitchen, filled the kettle, then set it down and continued toward the liquor cabinet. She knew she must look hideous, like a disheveled old crone out of a Brothers Grimm story.

Which meant Justin was winning, she realized with a scowl. He was bulldozing her to the abyss of madness, where she would sign whatever he wanted and then slink away, grateful for the few crumbs he'd given her. She couldn't even be sure she'd get Puddy back if she complied with his demands. He had been ruthless in his business affairs, and he'd never once had a kind word for Puddy. Her poor Puddy's body might be in a garbage bag at the curb in front of Justin's house, soon to be interred in the city dump.

Eloise banged down the glass. "I will not allow him to win," she said, spitting out each word with such anger that a haze of venom seemed to fill the room. She called her beauty shop, demanded an immediate appointment, and then carefully dressed, combed her hair, and applied lipstick and a faint dusting of blusher to disguise her pallor.

As she drove toward the center of town, she became increasingly bewildered by the expressions of pedestrians, as well as those in other vehicles. Women stared at her in horror, while men mouthed vulgarities and made unseemly gestures. A teenaged girl clapped her hand to mouth and sank to her knees on the sidewalk. A small child pointed at Eloise's car and screamed.

Eloise knew she'd been exaggerating when she described herself as a disheveled old crone, but she was beginning to wonder if she looked much worse than the image she'd seen in her mirror. Was there some sort of invisible stigma attached to a middle-aged woman who'd been discarded by her husband? Before leaving her house, she'd checked the car for any sort of vandalism, from a swastika spray-painted on the passenger side to obscene bumper stickers. Experience had taught her caution in such matters.

She could think of nothing to do but continue on her way, despite the revulsion she was leaving in her wake. She'd just turned the corner when she saw blue lights flashing in the rearview mirror and heard the momentary burp of a siren. She pulled over obediently and forced herself to assume a demeanor of expectancy and the slightest trace of self-righteousness as she watched the police officer emerge from his car.

To her surprise, he squatted down behind her car for a long moment. When he arose and came to her window, his expression was stony.

"You think that's funny, lady?" he said. "Well, you're the sickest damn practical joker I've had the displeasure to deal with. Driver's license and registration."

"I don't understand," Eloise said with as much civility as she could muster. "I was not exceeding the speed limit, and I am always careful about coming to a full stop at stop signs.

I've never had a traffic ticket in my life, except for the odd parking ticket."

"Yeah, right. I'm gonna have to radio in and find out what the violation is. License and registration—now."

Eloise handed over the pertinent documentation, adding her proof of insurance to emphasize her willingness to cooperate, then sank back as the officer returned to his car. Why was she being treated with this unmistakable contempt?

She was startled out of her reverie when a woman pushing a stroller glared at her and said, "You make me want to puke."

Eloise got out of the car and blinked at the woman, who mutely pointed at the back of the car. There on the asphalt, attached by a rope tied under the bumper, lay a bedraggled stuffed toy sprinkled with red paint. At a distance, Eloise realized, as her stomach knotted with disgust, it looked very much like a dead cat.

"Oh, my God," she said, fighting for breath and oblivious to the tears streaming down her cheeks. "I didn't know it was there. What must everyone have thought of me? I would never harm a cat! You must believe me! I'm not—not like that."

She sat down in the car and dully waited for the officer to return. When he finally did, she explained rather inarticulately that this was a cruel joke played upon her by her estranged husband and then, regaining control of herself, made sure the officer wrote down Justin's name and that of the Lincoln-Mercury dealership.

The officer nodded solemnly. "We get some pretty strange calls when people are divorcing, but this is the nastiest trick I've heard of. You want me to untie the rope?"

She did, of course, and when the evidence had been put in her trunk, she turned around and drove home. After a glass of gin took the knots out of her stomach, she donned gloves and wrote anonymous letters to the homeowners in Justin's new neighborhood, warning them that he was a convicted child molester. Then, feeling steadier, she called all the cemeteries in town and made evening appointments for Kelli so that she and Justin could explore the possibility of spending eternity in adjoining slots. Inspiration struck, and she called all the funeral homes and arranged for representatives to drop by and assist the lovebirds in preplanning their funerals.

Although the activity was satisfying, it did little to erase the dreadful image of the stained toy cat with the rope around its neck. It was obviously a threat against Puddy, held captive and no doubt being abused and neglected. Would she find him at the end of the next rope?

Again she found it impossible to sleep, and by the next morning she was so exhausted that she could barely focus on her surroundings. The furniture seemed unfamiliar, the walls bulging, the windows presenting a surreal picture of her yard. The telephone rang several times during the day, but Eloise could only stare at it.

By nine o'clock that night the gin bottle was empty, as were the sherry, scotch, and vermouth bottles. Eloise was trying to coax the last olive out of the jar when the doorbell chimed. She sat where she was, paralyzed at the possibility that she might find herself confronting Milt or even one of her treacherous friends. Then she remembered the posters she had put up offering a reward for Puddy's return and stumbled to her feet.

No one was waiting on the porch, nor was there a second envelope on the doormat. What she did see was a box, six inches square, with printing on its side. She gingerly picked it up and read the swirling words: Memorial Funeral Home and Crematorium.

She looked wildly at the empty sidewalk, then stepped back inside and locked the door. Her hands trembled violently as she forced open the box. Inside was a small brass urn with decorative etching and inlaid mother-of-pearl flowers. Biting her lip, she opened the lid and gazed at the soft gray ashes.

At that point, automatic pilot took over. She placed the urn on the coffee table, picked up her purse, and went out to the garage to find the three-gallon gas can left by the yardmen. She drove to the gas station and managed to fill the can at the pump, then continued to Justin's house in the posh neighborhood on the top of the hill.

There were no lights shining from the downstairs floor, but a glow came through drawn drapes in a second-floor room and she could hear what she thought was a television show.

She soaked the porch with gasoline, then went around to the deck at the back of the house and did the same. She dropped a lit match, returned to the front of the house and did the same, and watched until flames began to leap like devilish ballerinas.

Her task completed, Eloise drove home. She had no delusions that she would not be apprehended and charged with arson. She could only hope that first-degree murder would be added once the ruins had been sifted.

She was seated in the living room, cradling the urn and reminiscing about Puddy's days as a mischievous kitten, when the doorbell chimed. So soon, she thought as she set the urn on the mantel and prepared herself to face the consequences of her actions.

A nervous woman, vaguely familiar, stood on the porch. "Mrs. Bainbury, I live down at the corner across from the park, and I want you to know how sorry I am."

"Sorry?" echoed Eloise.

"Four nights ago we got a call that my father had had a heart attack. I bundled everybody into the car and drove all night to get to the hospital. It turned out not to be all that serious, but we stayed to help my mother get through the ordeal. When we arrived home less than an hour ago, I opened the garage door and saw a large yellow cat shoot out and disappear into the shrubbery. My son recognized it as yours, and the poster on the telephone pole confirmed it. I suppose he must have been locked in the garage all this time. I'm really, really sorry."

"These things do happen, don't they?" murmured Eloise. She was going to offer a word or two of sympathy for the woman's father when she saw a police car coming down the street. "If you'll excuse me," she said, "I need to make sure Puddy finds fresh kibble and water on his return. Thank you so much for coming by."

When the police car pulled into her driveway, Eloise was in the yard, sprinkling ashes on the rose bed. Ashes added important nutrients to the soil, she thought with a smile. The roses would be glorious by the end of the summer.

Dead on Arrival

The girl's body lay in the middle of my living room floor. Long, black hair partially veiled her face and wound around her neck like a silky scarf. Her hands were contorted, her eyes flat and unfocused. The hilt of a knife protruded from her chest, an unadorned wooden marker in an irregular blotch of blood.

For a long, paralytic minute, all I did was stare, trying to convince myself that I was in the throes of some obscure jet lag syndrome that involved a particularly insidious form of hallucination. I finally dropped my suitcase, purse, nylon carry-on bag, and sack of groceries I'd bought on the way from the airport, stuck my knuckles in my mouth, and edged around the sofa for a closer look.

It was not a good idea. I stumbled back, doing my best not to scream or swoon or something equally unproductive, and made it to the telephone in the kitchen. I thought I'd managed to avoid hysterics, but by the time Peter came on the line, my voice was an octave too high and I was slumped on the floor with my back against a cabinet door.

"There's a body in the living room," I said.

"Claire? Are you all right?"

"No, I am not all right, but I'm a damn sight better than

that poor girl in the living room, because she's dead and I'm going to scream any minute and you'd—"

"I thought you were in Atlanta at that booksellers' convention until Thursday?"

"Well, I'm not," I said unsteadily and perhaps a shade acerbically. "I got home about three minutes ago, and there's this body in the living room and I'd appreciate it if you'll stop behaving like a nosy travel agent and do something because I really, truly am going to lose control—"

"Get out of there," Peter cut in harshly. "No! Go downstairs and wait until we get there."

I dropped the receiver and gazed down the hall at my bedroom door, Caron's bedroom, and the bathroom door. All three were closed. I looked up at the back door, which was bolted from the inside. I listened intently for a sound, a faint intake of breath or the merest scuffle of a nervous foot. Or a bellow from a maniacal monster with a bad attitude and another knife.

It took several seconds of mental lecturing to get myself up, out of the kitchen and back through the living room, where I kept my eyes on the front door with the determination of a dieter passing a bakery or a mild-mannered bookseller passing a corpse. I then ran down the steps to the ground floor apartment and pounded on the door in a most undignified fashion. I was prepared to beat it down with my fists if need be when the lock clicked and the door opened a few inches, saving me countless splinters and an unpleasant conversation with the miserly landlord.

"Mrs. Malloy?" said a startled voice. "I thought you were in Atlanta for another couple of days."

The apartment had been rented a few weeks earlier to two college boys with the unremarkable names of Jonathon and Sean. I hadn't bothered to figure out which was which, and at the moment I still wasn't interested.

"I am not in Atlanta. Let me in, please. There's been an—an accident upstairs. There may be someone hiding up there. The police are coming. I need to stay here."

"The police?" he said as he opened the door and gestured for me to come in. Jonathon (I thought) was a tall boy with blue eyes and stylish blond hair. At the moment his hair was dripping on the floor like melting icicles and he was clutching a towel around his waist. "I was taking a shower," he explained in case I was unable to make the leap unassisted. "Police, huh? I guess I'd better put some clothes on."

"Good idea." I sank down on a nubby Salvation Army sofa and rubbed my face, fighting not to visualize the body ten feet above my head. In my living room. Partly on the area rug.

"I'll tell Sean to get you something to drink," Jonathon continued, still attempting to play the gracious host in his towel.

He went into one of the bedrooms, and after a minute the other boy appeared. Sean moved slowly, his dark hair ruffled and his expression groggy. "Hi, Mrs. Malloy," he said through a yawn. "I was taking a nap. I stayed up all night because of a damn calculus exam this morning. Jon said the police are coming. That's weird, real weird. You want a glass of wine? I think we got some left from a party last weekend."

Before I could decline, sirens whined in the distance, becoming louder as they neared the usually quiet street across from the campus lawn. Blue light flashed, doors slammed, feet thudded on the porch, and voices barked like angry mastiffs. The Farberville cavalry, it seemed, had arrived.

Several hours later I was allowed to sit on my own sofa. The chalk outline on the other side of the coffee table looked like a crude paper-doll, and I tried to keep my eyes away from it. Peter Rosen of the Farberville CID, a man of great charm upon occasion, alternated between scribbling in his notebook and rubbing my neck.

"You're sure you didn't recognize her?" he said for not the first time.

"I'm very, very sure. Who was she? How did she get into my apartment, Peter?"

"We checked, and the deadbolt hasn't been tampered with. You've said several times now that you've got the only key and the door was locked when you came upstairs."

I leaned back and stared at the network of cracks in the ceiling. "When I got to the porch, I had to put everything down to unlock that door. I then put the key between my lips, picked everything up and trudged upstairs to my landing, where I had to put everything down again to unlock this door. It was locked; I'm sure of it."

"Caron doesn't have a key?"

"No one else has a key—not even the landlord. He had someone put on the deadbolts about five years ago and told me that I'd have to pay for a replacement if I lost my key. I considered having a copy made for Caron, but never got around to it. The only key is right there on the coffee table."

We both glared at the slightly discolored offender. When it failed to offer any hints, Peter opted to nuzzle my ear and murmur about the stupidity of citizens dallying in their scene-of-the-crime apartments when crazed murderers might be lurking in closets or behind closed doors.

The telephone rang, ending that nonsense. To someone's consternation, Peter took the call in the kitchen. Luckily, someone could overhear his side despite his efforts to mutter, and I was frowning when he rejoined me.

"Her name was Wendy, right?" I said. "I can't think of

anyone I've ever known named Wendy. Well, one, but I doubt she and a boy in green tights flew through an upstairs window."

"Wendy Billingsberg, a business major at the college. She was twenty-two and lived alone on the top floor of that cheap brick apartment house beside the copy shop. She was from some little town about forty miles from here called Hasty. Her family's being notified now, and I suppose I'll question them tomorrow when they've had a chance to assimilate this. It's even harder when the victim is young." He looked away for a moment. "Wendy Billingsberg. Perhaps she came into the Book Depot. Try to remember if you've seen the name on a check or a credit card."

I did as directed, then shook my head. "I make the students produce a battery of identification, and I think I'd remember the name. I did look at her face when they—took her out. She was a pretty girl and that long black hair was striking. I can't swear she's never been in the bookstore or walked past me on the sidewalk, but I'm almost certain I never spoke to her, Peter. Why was she in my apartment and how did she get inside?"

Peter flipped through his notebook and sighed. "The medical examiner said the angle of the weapon was such that the wound could not have been self-inflicted, so she wasn't the only one here."

"What about the two boys downstairs? Have they ever seen her before, or noticed her hanging around the neighborhood?"

"Jorgeson had them look at the victim and then interviewed them briefly. Neither one recognized her or offered any theory concerning what she was doing in your apartment. Could she have been a friend of Caron's?"

"I don't think so," I said, then went to the telephone, dialed Inez's number, and asked to speak to Caron.

She responded with the customary grace of a fifteen-year-old controlled solely by hormonal tides. "What, Mother? Inez and I were just about to go over to Rhonda's house to watch a movie. Aren't you supposed to be in Atlanta?"

"Yes, I am supposed to be in Atlanta," I said evenly, "but I am not. I am home and this is important. Do you know a twenty-two-year-old girl named Wendy Billingsberg?"

"No. Is that all? Inez and I really, really need to go now. Rhonda's such a bitch that she won't bother to wait for us. Some people have no consideration." Her tone made it clear there was more than one inconsiderate person in her life.

I reported the gist to Peter, who sighed again and said he'd better return to the police station to see if Jorgeson had dug up anything further. He promised to send by a uniformed officer to install a chain until I could have the lock rekeyed, and then spent several minutes asking my earlobes if I would be all right.

We all assured him I would, but after he'd gone, I caught myself tiptoeing around the apartment as I unpacked groceries and put away my suitcase. The front door had been locked; the back door had been bolted from the inside. The locks on the windows were unsullied except for a patina of black dust from being examined for fingerprints. They were not the only things to have been dusted, of course. Most of the surfaces in the apartment had been treated in a similar fashion, and had produced Caron's prints all over everything (including the bottle of perfume Peter'd given me for my birthday), mine, and one on a glass on the bedside table that had resulted in a moment of great excitement, until Peter suggested they compare it to his. The success of this resulted in a silence and several smirky glances.

Wendy and her companion had not searched the apartment. There was no indication they'd gone further than the living room. Why had they chosen my apartment—and how had they gotten inside?

An idea struck, and I hurried into the kitchen and hunted through junky drawers until I found the telephone number of my landlord. I crossed my fingers as I dialed the number, and was rewarded with a grouchy hello. "Mr. Fleechum," I said excitedly, "this is Claire Malloy. I need to ask you something."

"Look, I told you when you moved in that I didn't want any damn excuses about the rent. I ain't your father, and I don't care about your financial problems. I got to pay the bank every month, so there's no point in—"

"That's not why I called," I interrupted before he worked himself into an impressive fettle. "I was hoping you might remember the name of the locksmith who installed the deadbolts several years ago . . ."

"Yeah, I know his name. You lose the key, Mizz Malloy? I told you then that I wasn't going to waste money on a spare."

I wasn't inclined to explain the situation at the moment. "No, I didn't lose the key. I was thinking about having a deadbolt installed on the back door—at my expense, naturally. My daughter and I would feel more secure."

Fleechum grumbled under his breath, then said, "That's all right with me, as long as I don't have to pay for it. But you'll have to find your own locksmith. My deadbeat brother-in-law put in the deadbolts, due in part to owing me money. He cleared out three, four years ago, taking his tools. My sister had everything else hauled off to the dump. I'm just sorry that sorry husband of hers couldn't have been in the bottom of the load."

"And no one knows where he is now?"

"No one cares where he is now, Mizz Malloy, including me. Last I heard he was in Arizona or some place like that,

living in a trailer with a bimbo. Probably beating her like he
did my sister. You want to have locks installed, do it."

He replaced the receiver with an unnecessary vigor. I put
mine down more gently and regretfully allowed my brilliant
idea to deflate like a cooling soufflé. Mr. Fleechum's
brother-in-law had been gone for three or four years. It
seemed unlikely that he had made an extra key, kept it all
that time, and then waited until my apartment was empty for
a few days so that he could invite a college girl over to
murder her.

I was still tiptoeing, but I couldn't seem to shake a sense of
someone or something hovering in the apartment, possessing
it in the tradition of a proper British ghost in the tower. I went
so far as to stand in the dining room doorway, trying to pick
up some psychic insight into an earlier scene when two people
had entered the room and one had departed.

I tried to envision them as burglars. They'd have been seriously disappointed burglars when they saw the decrepit
stereo system and small television set. But why choose my
apartment to begin with? The duplex fit in well with the
neighborhood ambiance of run-down rental property and
transient tenants. There were people downstairs, single boys
who were likely to come and go at unpredictable hours and
have a stream of visitors.

Okay, Wendy and her companion weren't burglars and
they hadn't come in hopes of filching the Hope Diamond and
other fancy stuff. The girl had come to see me, and her murderer had followed her, bringing his knife with him. She
hadn't known I was out of town—and why would she, since
she didn't know me from Mary Magdalen?

A knock on the door interrupted my admittedly pointless
mental exercise. It also knotted my stomach and threatened
my knees, and my voice was shaky as I said, "Who is it?"

"Jorgeson and Corporal Katz, Mrs. Malloy. Katz is going to put up the chain so you'll feel safe tonight."

I let them in. Katz immediately busied himself with screwdrivers and such, while Jorgeson watched with the impassiveness of a road-crew supervisor. I subtly sidled over and said, "Have you turned up anything more about the victim?"

"The lieutenant said not to discuss it with you, ma'am," Jorgeson said, his bulldog face turning pink. "He said that you're not supposed to meddle in an official police investigation—this time."

"Oh, Jorgeson," I said with a charmingly wry chuckle, "we both know the lieutenant didn't mean that I wasn't supposed to know anything whatsoever about the victim. I might be able to remember something if I knew more about her. What if she'd been a contestant in that ghastly beauty pageant I helped direct, or been a waitress at the beer garden across from the Book Depot? You know how awkward it is to run into someone you've seen a thousand times, but you can't place him because he's out of context. When I saw this Wendy Billingsberg, she was decidedly out of context."

Jorgeson's jaw crept out further and his ears gradually matched the hue of his face. "The lieutenant said you'd try something like that, ma'am. As far as we know, the victim didn't have any connections with any of the locals. She attended classes sporadically and pretty much hung out with the more unsavory elements of the campus community."

"Ah," I said wisely, "drugs." When Jorgeson twitched, I bit back a smile and continued. "Peter's right; none of the druggies buy books at the store or hold down jobs along Thurber Street. Was she dealing?"

"I'm not supposed to discuss it, ma'am. Hurry up, Katz. I told those boys downstairs to wait for me."

Katz hurried up, and within a few minutes, Jorgeson

wished me a nice day (and hadn't it been dandy thus far?) and led his cohort out of my apartment. I waited until I heard them reach the ground floor, then eased open my door and crept as close to the middle landing as I dared.

Jorgeson, bless his heart, had opted to conduct his interview from the foyer. "Wendy Billingsberg," he said in a low voice. "You both sure that doesn't ring a bell? She was a business major. Either of you have any classes in the department?" There was a pause during which I assumed they'd made suitable nonverbal responses. "She lived in the Bellaire Apartments. You been there?" Another pause. "And she used to be seen on the street with a coke dealer nicknamed Hambone. Tall guy, dirty blond ponytail, brown beard, disappeared at the end of the last semester, probably when he caught wind of a pending warrant. Ever heard of this Hambone?"

"Hambone?" Jonathon echoed. "The description doesn't sound like anyone I know, but we're not exactly in that social circle. What's his real name?"

"We're still working on that," Jorgeson said. "What about you? You ever heard of someone named Hambone?"

"Nope," Sean said firmly. "Look, Officer, I was up all night studying. I've already told you that I didn't see anyone and I didn't hear anything."

"Neither did I," Jonathon said with equal conviction. "I went out for a hamburger and a brew at the beer garden, then came back and watched some old war movie. Fell asleep on the couch."

"What time did you leave and subsequently return?" Jorgeson asked, still speaking softly but with an edge of intensity.

"Jesus, I don't know. I went out at maybe ten and got back at maybe midnight. You can ask the chubby blond waitress; she's seen me enough times to remember me."

"The medical examiner's initial estimate is that the girl was killed around midnight, with an hour margin of error on either side. It looks like the girl and her friend managed to sneak upstairs while you were out and your roommate was studying in his bedroom. You didn't notice anyone on the sidewalk when you came back?"

After a pause, Jonathon said, "Well, there was a couple, but they were heading away from the duplex and having a heated discussion about him forgetting her birthday or something. I didn't pay much attention, and it was too dark to get a good look at them. Other than them, I don't think I saw anyone during the last couple of blocks. There was a guy going around the corner the other way, but all I saw was the back of his head."

"Did he have a ponytail?" Jorgeson said quickly.

"I just caught a glimpse of him. Sorry."

I heard the sound of Jorgeson's pencil scratching a brief note. "And you didn't hear anything?" he added, now speaking to the other boy.

"No," Sean said, "I've already told you that. Nothing."

"That's enough for the moment," Jorgeson said. "Both of you need to come to the station tomorrow morning so we can take formal statements. In the meantime, if you think of anything at all that might help, call Lieutenant Rosen or myself."

The front door closed. The downstairs door closed. Shortly thereafter, two car doors closed. I closed my door and tested the chain Katz had installed. It allowed the door to open two or three inches and seemed solid enough until I could get the lock rekeyed, which was pretty darn close to the top of my priorities list. Breathing, number one. Deadbolt rekeyed, number two.

I went into the kitchen, made sure the bolt on the back door was still in place, and started to make myself a cup of tea while I assimilated the latest information so graciously shared with me.

Wendy was known to have consorted with a dealer. He'd vanished, and no doubt preferred to remain thus. She'd run into him, recognized him, and threatened to expose him. She found a way into my apartment and ended up on the living room floor. I again checked the bolt, then turned off the burner beneath the tea kettle and made myself a nice, stiff drink. I went back into the living room, checked that the chain was in place and the deadbolt secured, and sat down on the sofa, wondering if the emergent compulsion to maintain security would be with me for weeks, months, or decades.

I put down my drink, checked that the chain and deadbolt had not slipped loose, and went into the kitchen to call a locksmith and pay for an after-hours emergency visit. And after a moment of revelation, found myself calling someone else.

Half an hour later I went downstairs and knocked on the boys' door. Jonathon opened the door. His expression tightened as he saw me, as though he expected another bizarre outburst from the crazy lady who cohabited with bats in the upstairs belfry.

"Hi," I said in a thoroughly civilized voice. "I realize it's been an awful day for all of us, but I'm not going to be able to relax, much less sleep, if I don't have the locksmith in to rekey the deadbolt. He said he'd be here in an hour. I just thought I'd warn you and Sean so you wouldn't come storming out the door."

"Sean's sacked out under the air conditioner, so he couldn't hear a freight train drive across the porch. I'll see if I can get through to him, though. We're both pretty rattled by all this. Thanks for telling me, but I think I'll wander down to the beer garden and soothe myself with a pitcher. Two pitchers. Whatever it takes."

I went back upstairs, secured the chain and the deadbolt, and sat down to wait. Ten minutes later I heard the front door downstairs close and footsteps on the porch. So far, so good. I turned on the television to give a sense of security to my visitor as he came creeping up the squeaky stairs, the key to my door in what surely was a very sweaty hand.

To my chagrin, it was all for naught, because he walked up the stairs like he owned them (or rented them, anyway) and knocked on my door.

"Who is it?" I said with the breathlessness of a gothic heroine.

"It's Sean, Mrs. Malloy. I wanted to talk to you for a minute. There's something that occurred to me, and I don't know if it's important enough to call the police now."

"Sorry," I said through the door, "but I'm too terrified to open the door to anyone except the locksmith. Go ahead and call Lieutenant Rosen; I'm sure he'll want to hear whatever you have."

I listened with increasing disappointment as he went downstairs and into his apartment. A window unit began to hum somewhere below.

"Phooey," I said as I switched off the television and did a quick round to ascertain all my locks were locked. I was brooding on the sofa several minutes later when I heard a telltale series of squeaks. A key rustled into the keyhole. As I stared, fascinated and rather pleased with myself, the knob of the lock clicked to one side, the doorknob twisted silently, and the door edged open. I went so far as to assume the standard gothic heroine stance: hands clasped beside my chest, eyelids frozen in mid-flutter, lips pursed.

Then the chain reached its limit, of course, and the door came to a halt. A male voice let out a muted grunt of frustration, but became much louder as the police came thundering upstairs. Once the arguing and protesting abated, I removed the chain and opened the door.

Jonathon had been handcuffed and was in the process of being escorted downstairs by Jorgeson and Katz, among others. Peter gave me a pained look and said, "I was about to remove the evidence from your lock when you did that, Claire. Why don't you wait inside like a good little girl?"

"Because I'm not," I said, now opting for the role of gothic dowager dealing with inferiors. "I happen to be the one who figured out the key problem, you know."

"You happen to be the one who swore there was only one key for the deadbolt. That's what threw me off in the first place."

"Don't pull that nonsense. You heard me say that I used the same key downstairs as upstairs. It was perfectly obvious that my door, the boys' door, and the front door are all keyed the same. Fleechum, the prince of penury, saved himself big bucks. Once I told the boys that a locksmith was coming, both of them realized they'd have to have their deadbolt rekeyed, too. Sean was puzzled, but I'm afraid Jonathon was panicked enough to try something unpleasant."

"It would have come to me at two in the morning," Peter said. "I would have sat up in bed, slapped my forehead, and called Jorgeson to rush over here and test the theory."

"Then I'm delighted that your sleep will be uninterrupted."

"When I get some, which won't be anytime soon. Now we've got to see if anyone at the beer garden noticed Wendy recognize her old boyfriend and follow him back to his apartment. Sean wouldn't have heard any discussion, but he might have had problems with a corpse in his living room the next morning. Did you tell the boys you'd be in Atlanta until Thursday?"

"I asked them to collect my mail."

"So Jonathon, a.k.a. Hambone, figured he had a couple of days to do something with the body. Unfortunately, you returned."

"Unfortunately, my fanny! If I hadn't come home early, he might have had a chance to take Wendy's body out in the woods where she wouldn't have been discovered for weeks. Months. Decades. And don't you find it a bit ironic that you sent me downstairs—to the murderer's apartment—when I discovered the body?" I was warming up for another onslaught of righteous indignation when Peter put his arms around me.

"And why did you come home early?" he murmured.

"Because every now and then I like being told that I'm a meddlesome busybody who interferes in official police investigations," I retorted, now warming up for entirely different reasons. "No one in Atlanta had anything but nice things to say about me."

"Are you saying you missed me?"

"Jorgeson, you fool," I said. "I missed Jorgeson."

I wondered if his soft laugh meant he didn't believe me.

The Last to Know

"Bambi's father was murdered last night," Caron announced as she sailed through the door of the Book Depot, tossed her bulky backpack on the counter, and continued toward my office, no doubt in hopes I had squirreled away a diet soda for what passed for high tea these days, in that scones were out of the question, and clotted cream merely a fantasy.

"Wait a minute," I said to her back. Although her birth certificate claimed we had an irrevocable biological tie, I'd wondered on more than one occasion if the gypsies hadn't pulled a fast one in the nursery. We both had red hair, freckles, green eyes, and a certain determination—in my case, mild and thoughtful; in hers, more like that of a bronco displeased with the unfamiliar and unwelcome weight of a cowboy with spurs.

She stopped and looked back, her nostrils flaring. "I am about to Die of Thirst, Mother. We have a substitute in gym class, and she's nothing but a petty tyrant, totally oblivious to pains and suffering. We had to play volleyball all period without so much as—"

"What did you say about Bambi's father? Was it some sort of obscure Disneyesque reference? Thumper developed rabies? Flower found an assault weapon amidst the buttercups?"

"I am drenched in sweat."

I told her where I'd hidden the soda, then sat on the stool behind the counter and gloomily gazed at the paperwork necessary to return several boxes of unsold books. The sales departments of publishing houses are more adept than the IRS at concocting a miasmatic labyrinth of figures, columns, and sly demands that can delay the process for months, if not years.

Caron returned with my soda and the insufferable smugness of a fifteen-year-old who knows she can seize center stage, if only for a few minutes. The reality that the center stage was in a dusty old bookstore patronized only by the few quasi-literates in Farberville did not deter her. "Not Bambi the geek deer," she said with a pitying smile for her witless mother. "Bambi McQueen, the senior who's editor of the school newspaper. Don't you remember her from when you substituted in the journalism department?"

It was not the moment to admit all high school students had a remarkably uninteresting sameness, from their clothes to their sulky expressions. "I think so," I said mendaciously. "What happened to her father?"

"It's so melodramatic." Caron paused to pop the top of the can, still relishing her ephemeral power. "It seems he was having an affair with Bambi's mother's best friend. The friend showed up at their house, tanked to the gills and screaming at him for dumping her, then said she was going to go home and kill herself." She paused again to slurp the soda and assess how much longer she could drag out the story. "Pretty dumb, if you ask me. I met him when Bambi had a Christmas party for the staff, and I was not impressed. He's okay-looking, but he's got—had—this prissy little mouth, and he was forever peering at us over the top of his glasses like we were nothing but a bunch of botched lobotomies swilling his expensive eggnog."

"What happened after the friend said she was going to kill herself?" I persisted.

"This is where it gets Utterly Gruesome. Mr. McQueen was really alarmed and followed her outside. She got in her car, but instead of leaving, she ran over him in the driveway and smashed him into the family station wagon like a bug on the windshield. She claimed her foot slipped, but the police aren't so sure." Caron dropped the empty can on the counter and made a grab for her backpack.

I caught her wrist. "That's a tragic story. Where'd you learn the details?"

"It's all over school. Bambi wasn't there today, naturally, but she called Emily at midnight, and Emily told practically everybody in the entire school. Emily's mouth should be in the Smithsonian—in a display case of its own." She removed my hand. "I have tons of homework, Mother. Unless you want me to like flunk out and do menial housework for the rest of my life, you'd better let me go to the library and look up stuff about boring dead presidents."

"I find it difficult to imagine your success as a cleaning woman, considering the sorry state of your closet and the collection of dirty dishes under your bed. By all means, run along to the library and do your homework. Afterwards, you may explore this new career option by cleaning up your room." Her snort was predictable, but I realized there was something that was not. "Where's Inez? Is she sick today?"

"I really couldn't say," Caron said coldly as she headed for the door. "I don't keep track of treacherous bitches."

I was blinking as the bell above the door jangled and the rigid silhouette of my daughter passed in front of the window. Inez Thornton was Caron's shadow, in every sense of the word. Not only did she trail after Caron like an indentured handservant, she did so in a drab, almost inanimate fashion that served as a perfect counterpart to Caron's general air of impending hysteria. Inez was burdened with the lingering softness of baby fat, thick-lensed glasses that gave her an owlish look, and a voice that rarely rose above a whisper, much less rattled the china. On days when Caron was a definitive raging blizzard, Inez was but a foggy spring morning.

And also, from this parting pronouncement, a treacherous bitch. "This, too, will pass," I murmured to myself as I bent down over the devil's own paperwork, determined to banish images of a splattered windshield until I could devise a way to convince a heartless sales department to restore my credit, however fleetingly.

That evening when I arrived in the upstairs duplex across from the lawn of Farber College, Caron's room was uninhabited by any life form more complex than the fuzzy blue mold on the plates under her bed. At the rate they were accumulating, full service for twelve would be available on her wedding day, saving her the tedium of bridal registration.

I closed the door, made myself a drink, and sank down on the sofa to peruse the local newspaper for the article concerning Bambi's father. On the second page I found a few paragraphs, thick with "allegedly" and "purportedly," that related how Charlene "Charlie" Kirkpatrick, longtime friend of Michelle McQueen, had contributed to the untimely demise of Ethan McQueen. Ms. Kirkpatrick would be arraigned as soon as she was released from the detoxification ward of the hospital, and Ms. McQueen was refusing to be interviewed. Mr. McQueen was survived by his wife and daughter of the home, his mother in a nearby town, and a sister in California. The funeral would be held Monday at two o'clock in the yuppiest Episcopal church, followed by a graveside service at the old cemetery only a few blocks from the Book Depot.

I put down the newspaper and tried to envision Bambi. It was too much like seeking to pinpoint one buffalo in a stampeding herd, which was how I'd described the denizens of the hallways of Farberville High School when I'd been coerced into substituting for doddery Miss Parchester, who'd been accused of embezzlement and murder.

I gave up on Bambi's face and turned on the six o'clock news. The death, accidental or intentional, was the lead story, of course, since Farberville was generally a dull place, its criminal activity limited to brawls among the students, armed robberies at the convenience stores, and mundane burglaries. Although the story struck me as nothing more lurid than domestic violence of the worst sort, the anchorman had a jolly time droning on while we were treated to footage of a bloodstained driveway and the battered hood of a station wagon.

Footsteps pounded up the stairs, interspersed with strident voices and bitterly sardonic laughter. Odds were good that it wasn't Peter Rosen, the police lieutenant with whom I'd become embroiled after a distasteful investigation involving the murder of a local romance writer. He was unnervingly handsome, in a hawkish way, and invariably maddening when he scolded me for my brilliant insights into subsequent cases. We were both consenting adults, and indeed consented in ways that left me idly considering the possibility of a permanent liaison. Dawn would break, however, and so would my resolve to give up my reservations about marriage, about dividing the closet, about facing him at breakfast every morning, about assigning him a pillow, and about relinquishing my life as a competent, marginally self-supporting single woman.

Caron stomped into my reverie, her eyes flashing and her

mouth curled into a smirk. On her heels was a girl who was briskly introduced as Melissa-from-biology, who bobbled her head indifferently and allowed herself to be led to Caron's room.

"Can you believe Inez is actually spending the night at Rhonda's tomorrow?" Caron said, slathering the sentence with condemnation. "I suspected all along that she was using me so she could cozy up with the cheerleaders. I felt sorry for her because she's so nerdy, but that doesn't like give her the right to—"

Caron's bedroom door closed on whatever right Inez had dared to exercise.

Hoping that Melissa-from-biology was up on her tetanus shots, I made myself another drink, watched the rest of the news and the weather report, and was settled in with a mystery novel when I heard more decorous steps outside the door. I admitted Peter, who greeted me with great style and asked with the quivery optimism of Oliver Twist for a beer. His face was stubbly, and there were darkish crescents under his molasses brown eyes. His usually impeccable three-piece suit was wrinkled, and a coffee stain marred the silk tie I'd given him for his birthday.

Once I'd complied with a beer, I curled up next to him and said, "You look like hell, darling. Were you up all night with this tragedy in the McQueen driveway?"

He glowered briefly at the newspaper I'd inadvertently left folded to the pertinent page. "All night, and most of today," he admitted with a sigh. "Not that we're dealing with something bizarre enough to warrant a true crime novel and a three-part miniseries. The victim's midlife crisis resulted in his death, the destruction of the lives of two women who have been best friends since college, and who knows what kind of psychological problems in the future for the daughter.

Married men really shouldn't have affairs." One hand slid around my waist, and the other in a more intimate direction as he nuzzled my neck. "Neither should single men. They should get married and settle down in domestic tranquility with someone who's undeniably attractive, well-educated, intelligent, meddlesome, and incredibly delightful and innovative in bed."

I removed my neck from his nuzzle. "If you tell me about the case, I'll heat up last night's pizza."

"Are you bribing a police officer?"

"I think there are at least three slices, presuming Caron didn't detour through the kitchen on her way to the library," I countered with said child's smugness, aware that the way to a cop's investigation was through his stomach.

He fell for it, and once I'd carried out my half of the bargain, he gulped down a piece with an apologetic look, wiped tomato sauce off his chin, and said, "Charlie Kirkpatrick and Michelle McQueen met in college, where they were roommates for four years. Both eventually married. Michelle stayed here, and Charlie lived in various other places for the next fifteen or so years. They kept in touch with calls and letters, however, and when Charlie divorced her husband five years ago, she moved back here and bought a house around the corner from the McQueens. Her son's away at college, and her daughter's married and lives in Chicago."

"And?" I said encouragingly.

"She and Michelle resumed their friendship—to the point that Ethan McQueen began to object, according to the daughter. Charlie worked at a travel agency, and was always inviting Michelle to come with her on inexpensive or even free trips. They went to the movies, had lunch several times a week, played golf on Wednesday mornings, and worked on the same charity fund-raisers. Charlie ate dinner with them often, and brunch every Sunday."

"What was the husband like? Caron met him and dismissed him as a prissy-mouthed judge, but she's of an age that anyone who doesn't fawn all over her is obviously demented."

"He was a moderately successful lawyer," Peter said. "He was past president of the county bar, involved in local politics, possibly in line for a judgeship in a few years. He played poker with the guys, drove a damned expensive sports car, patted his secretary on the fanny, seduced female clients, all that sort of lawyer thing."

"Including having an affair with his wife's best friend? Have I been underestimating the profession?"

"Michelle says she began to suspect as much about six months ago. She couldn't bring herself to openly confront either of them, although she did break off her relationship with Charlie. Said she couldn't bear to pretend to chatter over lunch when she was envisioning the two of them in a seedy motel room. Last night her suspicions were confirmed."

"What will happen to Charlie?"

"She'll be arraigned in the morning. The prosecuting attorney's talking second-degree murder at the moment, maybe thinking he can get a jury to go for manslaughter. There's no question that Charlie Kirkpatrick was in a state of extreme emotional disturbance; the wife was able to give us a detailed picture of what happened."

Peter put down his plate and tried a diversionary tactic involving my earlobe, but I made it clear I wasn't yet ready for such nonsense. Retrieving his plate, he added, "If the wife repeats her story on the witness stand, the prosecutor knows damn well he'll lose. We already know Charlie had more than enough alcohol in her blood to stop a much larger man in his tracks, and she was incoherent. We're subpoenaing records from her psychiatrist. What's likely to happen is that Charlie will plead guilty to negligent homicide, a class A misdemeanor. She'll receive a fine and no more than a year in the county jail, and be out within three months. If her lawyer's really sharp, she may end up with nothing more annoying than a suspended sentence and a couple of hundred hours of community service."

"Not exactly hard labor in the state's gulag," I said, shaking my head. "If she and Michelle were so close for twenty years, why would she have an affair with her best friend's husband? Unless she's completely devoid of morals it seems like he'd be her last choice."

"The ways of lust are as mysterious as that charming little freckle just below your left ear," he said. In that I'd gotten as much as I could from him, I allowed him to investigate at his leisure.

Nothing of interest happened over the weekend. Caron continued to hang around with Melissa-from-biology, carping and complaining about Inez's defection to the enemy camp. The general of that camp was Rhonda Maguire, who'd committed the unspeakable sin of snagging Louis Wilderberry, junior varsity quarterback and obviously so bewildered by Rhonda's slutty advances that he was unable to appreciate Caron's more delicate charm and vastly superior intellect.

The extent of Inez's treachery spread like an oil slick on what previously had been a pristine bay: spending Friday night with Rhonda, shopping at the mall the following day, being the first to hear the details of Rhonda's Saturday night date, and actually having the nerve to tell Emily that she felt sorry for Caron for being a moonstruck cow over Louis.

As for the tragedy at the McQueen house, less and less was found worthy to be aired on the evening news or reported in the newspaper. The station wagon was impounded and the driveway hosed down. The arraignment was delayed until Monday, while the doctors monitored Charlie Kirkpatrick's condition, and the prosecuting attorney pondered his alternative. Michelle McQueen and her daughter remained inside the house, admitting only family members and a casserole-bearing group of Episcopalian women.

Sunday afternoon I called my best friend, Luanne Bradshaw, and we talked for a long time about the McQueen case. Our relationship lacked parallel, in that I was widowed and she divorced; but we did agree that it was perplexing to imagine being so enamored of a mere man that one was willing to throw away a perfectly decent friendship.

Monday morning took an ugly turn. Caron stomped into the kitchen, jerked open the refrigerator to glare at an innocent pitcher of orange juice, and said, "I want to go to the funeral this afternoon. You'll have to check me out at noon so I can come home and change for it."

"Why do you want to go to the funeral? Bambi's hardly a close friend of yours, and it didn't sound as if you were fond of her father."

"Bambi is the editor of the school paper, Mother. Everybody else on the staff will be there. Do you want me to be the only one who Can't Bother to be there for Bambi?"

"Does this have anything to do with gym class?"

She slammed the refrigerator door. "I am trying to show some compassion, for pity's sake! After all, I do happen to know what it feels like when your father's accused of having an affair and then dies. Everyone gossips about it. Poor Bambi's going to have to come back to school and pretend she doesn't hear it, but she'll know when all of a sudden people clam up when she joins them, and she'll know they're staring at her when she walks down the hall."

It was a cheap shot, but a piercing one, and I acknowledged as much by arranging to meet her in the high school office at noon. I was by no means convinced the tyrannical gym teacher was not the primary motive for this untypical display of compassion and empathy, but it wouldn't hurt Caron to suffer through a funeral service in lieu of fifty relentless minutes of volleyball.

Peter called me at the Book Depot later in the morning to ask if I might be interested in a movie that evening. After I'd forced him to tell me that Charlie Kirkpatrick had been arraigned on charges of second-degree murder and then released on her own recognizance, I granted that I might enjoy a movie, and we settled on a time. I may not have mentioned that Caron and I were planning to go to Ethan McQueen's funeral, but it was nothing more than a minor omission, an excusable lapse of memory on the part of a nearly forty-year-old mind. I was attending it only because Caron was not yet old enough to drive, and I was unwilling to sit in the car outside the church, I assured myself. And perhaps I was just a bit curious to see the woman whose best friend had killed her husband. Prurient, but true, and a helluva lot more interesting than the stack of muddled invoices and overdue bills on the counter.

Nevertheless, I righteously waded through them until it was time to fetch Caron and go by the apartment to change into our funeral attire. After a spirited debate about which of us was to drive, the individual with the learner's permit flounced around to the passenger's side and flung herself into the seat with all the attractiveness of a thwarted toddler.

"Are things any better between you and Inez?" I asked as I hunted for a parking place in the lot behind the church. There were so many shiny new Mercedes and Beamers that it resembled a dealer's lot, but my crotchety old hatchback slid nicely into a niche by the dumpster.

"Hardly," Caron said, her voice as tight as my panty hose. "If she wants to spend all her time with Rhonda Maguire, I really don't see that it concerns me. Melissa may be dim, but at least she's loyal."

"Would it help if I spoke to her?"

"That'd be swell, Mother. She'll tell Rhonda and her catty friends, and I'll Absolutely Die. There's no way I could show my face at school ever again, and you can't afford one of those snooty, genderless boarding schools for the socially inept."

On that note, we went into the church and found seats for the requiem mass for Ethan McQueen, who was, according to the obituary within a pamphlet, a beloved son, brother, father, and husband. The church was crowded, and the only view I had of the grieving widow was that of soft brown hair and a taut neck. There were a lot of high school students present, and I caught myself wondering how many of them had gym class in the afternoon. It was not a charitable thought, but the mass was impersonal and interminable, and my curiosity unrequited.

"I can't wait to get out of these shoes," I said as Caron and I started for my car.

Her lower lip shot out. "We have to go to the cemetery. Everybody else is going, including the creepy little freshmen with acne for brains, and I don't want to be the only person on the entire staff of the *Falcon Crier* who's so mean-spirited that—"

I cut her off with an admission of defeat. We waited until the hearse and limousines were ready, and joined in the turtlish procession along Thurber Street to the cemetery. Parking was more difficult, and we ended up nearly two blocks from the canvas roof shielding the family from the incongruously bright sunshine.

"Over there," Caron muttered as she nudged me along like a petulant Bo Peep.

I looked at the family seated in chairs alongside the grave. Bambi was familiar; I had an indistinct memory of a simpery voice and well-developed deviousness. Her mother was rather ordinary, with an attractive face and an aura of composure despite an occasional dab with a tissue or a whispered word to Bambi and the white-haired matron on her other side.

We took our position at the back of a crowd of students, most of them shuffling nervously, the boys uncomfortable in suits and ties, the girls covertly appraising one another's dresses and jewelry. I was trying to peer over them to determine when the show would start when a hand tapped my shoulder.

"Hi, Mrs. Malloy," Inez whispered.

"Inez, how nice to see you," I said, then waited to see how Caron would react. She did not so much as quiver.

"This is Emily Cartigan," Inez continued with her typical timidity, blinking as if anticipating a slap. Emily nodded at me, arched her eyebrows at Caron's steely back, and drew Inez toward the perfidious Rhonda Maguire and a neckless boy wearing a letter jacket over his white shirt and dark tie.

I stole a peek at Caron, fully prepared to see steam coming from not only her ears, but also her nostrils and whatever other orifices were available. To my surprise, she had a vaguely triumphant smile as she gazed steadily at the dandruff-dotted shoulders of the boy in front of us.

The graveside service was brief, its major virtue. Very few people seemed inclined to approach the family, and those who did spoke only a word or two before fleeing. I could not imagine myself murmuring how sorry I was that the deceased had been killed by his mistress, and suggested to Caron that we forgo the ritual and go home to change clothes.

"I'll be there later," she said with a guileless look. "I want to stop by my father's grave for a few minutes and see how the plastic flowers are holding up."

"You do?" I had to take a breath to steady myself. "That's a lovely idea, dear. Would you like me to go with you, or wait in the car?"

"No, it may take a long time. I'll be home later, and then I've got to go to Melissa's house so we can work on this really mindless algebra assignment."

She took off on a gravel path that wound among the solitary stones and cozy family plots enclosed by low fences, her walk rather bouncy for someone on what some of us felt was a depressing mission. As she reached a bend, she looked over her shoulder, although not at me, and disappeared behind a row of trees.

Car doors slammed as the mourners began to depart. Bambi sat talking to her mother, who shook her head vehemently. After a moment, Bambi shrugged and stood up, and escorted her grandmother to the baby blue limousine. The preacher handed Michelle a Bible, held her hand for a moment, and walked toward his car with the obligatory introverted expression of the professionally bereaved. Michelle remained in the chair, her hands folded in her lap and her head lowered.

I walked toward my car, wishing I'd tucked more sensible shoes in my purse in anticipation of the distance. The gravel was not conducive to steady progress in even moderately sensible low heels, and I was lamenting the emergence of at least one blister when I saw a figure partially shielded by an unkempt hedge. Despite her sunglasses and a scarf, I recognized her from an earlier newscast when she'd been transferred from the hospital to the county jail. I had no doubt I could confirm the identification when the evening news covered her arraignment in a few hours.

It was curious, but so was my accountant when I tried to report financial quarterly estimates. I reopened the Book Depot, sold a paperback to my pet science fiction weirdo, and tried to reimmerse myself in paperwork, but I was distracted as much by the idea of Caron visiting her father's grave as I was by the image of Charlie Kirkpatrick observing the graveside service from behind the hedge. I finally pushed aside the ledger, propped my elbows on the counter, and, cradling my face in the classic pose of despondency, thought long and hard about the nature of friendship . . . not only between Michelle and Charlie, but also between Caron and Inez.

A theory began to emerge, and I called Luanne. "Would you have had an affair with Carlton?" I asked abruptly, bypassing pleasantries when thinking of my former husband.

"Not on a bet. From what you've said about him, he was a pompous pseudo-intellectual with an anal-retentive attitude about everything from meat loaf to movies."

"Did I say all that?"

"I am astute."

"I am impressed with your astutity—if that's a word."

"Not in my dictionary. If that's all, I just received a consignment from Dallas, some really nifty beaded dresses. I need to inventory the lot."

I rubbed my face. "Hold on a minute, Luanne. What if Carlton had been more like . . . say, Robert Redford. Would you have had an affair in spite of our friendship?"

"And when he dumped me, drive to your house and run him down in the driveway? Is that your point?" I made a noise indicating that it was, and after a moment of thought, she said, "No, but I'd be seriously tempted. You know how I feel about blue eyes and shaggy blond hair."

"Even sprinkled with gray?"

"I assume you're making rude remarks about his hair, but I wouldn't mind if his eyes were sprinkled with gray. I must count beads. Talk to you later."

I replaced the receiver and resumed staring blankly at the cracked plaster above the self-help rack. Luanne had answered honestly. She wouldn't have betrayed me, although the leap from Carlton to Robert required the imagination of a flimflam artist and the thighs of an aerobics instructor. Ethan to Robert was equally challenging.

Some women would, and had done so since the monosyllabic hunter had run into his distaff chum posing coyly in a scanty mastodon stole. But those weren't the women who had deep and long-lasting friendships with other women. They lacked the essential mechanism to bond, and most of us had learned to spot them quickly and clutch our men's arms possessively when they approached to poach.

I hung the fly-splattered Closed sign on the door, locked up, and let myself out the back door. I then unlocked the door and went inside to find the McQueens' address in the telephone directory. I was still clad in funerary finery, and I hoped I would be inconspicuous in the crowd of lawyers, their spouses, and whoever else was there.

Nobody was there. There was not one blessed car parked out front, not one mourner visible in the living room window, with a cocktail in hand and misty stories about good ol' Ethan. Wishing Luanne were beside me to dissuade me, I forced myself to go onto the porch and ring the doorbell.

Bambi opened the door and gave me a puzzled look through red, puffy eyes. "You're Caron Malloy's mother, right? You subbed for Miss Parchester for a few days when she was trying to poison everybody in the teacher's lounge."

"Something like that," I murmured. "I came by to offer you and your mother my condolences. This has been such a terrible time for you, and all I can say is that I'm really sorry. If there's anything Caron can do for you . . . ?"

"She's like a sophomore," said Bambi, clearly appalled at the concept. "Thanks, but no thanks. Listen, it was nice of you to come by, and I'll pass along the message to my mother when she gets back."

"From the cemetery?"

"Yeah, she was afraid those howling reporters would be here, and she said she wanted to be alone while she tried to understand how . . . Charlie could have done what she did."

"They were really close friends, weren't they?"

"That's what's killing her, she says. They've stayed in touch since college. When Charlie was married, she and my mother didn't talk on the phone every week, but they called at holidays and wrote a lot and sent funny cards and stuff like that. We visited them when they rented a beach house."

"She must have been thrilled when Charlie moved to Farberville and they could see more of each other," I said encouragingly, telling myself I was allowing Bambi to express her grief and confusion—rather than interrogating her four hours after her father's funeral.

"I suppose so." Bambi stepped back as if to close the door, but I opted to interpret it as a gesture of welcome and came into the entry hall. "Like I said, Mrs. Malloy, I'll tell my mother you came by," she said with an uneasy smile, "but it's about time for me to pick her up and—"

I radiated warmth like a veritable space heater. "Of course it is, dear, and I know you're not in the mood for visitors. I'll be off in a minute or two. From what I've heard, your mother began to suspect the two were having an affair about six months ago." I clucked my tongue disapprovingly.

Bambi conceded with a sigh, unable to withstand the persistence of dedicated meddler. "Right after they came back from a weekend at some bed-and-breakfast in Eureka Springs, they stopped seeing each other. My mother just said she'd learned disturbing things about Charlie and didn't want to be around her anymore. I think my father was secretly pleased that she didn't call all the time or show up Sunday mornings with cinnamon rolls and the newspapers. He seemed happier, but maybe it was because he and Charlie were—you know. Everybody in town knows, so why wouldn't you?" Her eyes brimmed with tears and her hands curled into fists. "Everybody at school knows, along with everybody at church and everybody at the goddamn grocery store! They probably knew the entire time." The tears spilled down her cheeks, but she ignored them with fierceness well beyond her years. "I guess that stupid saying is true—my mother was the last to know."

"One final question," I said despite the guilt that was gushing inside me and threatening to choke my despicable throat. "Were you here the night of the . . . accident?"

"No, I was over at Emily's house cramming for history. My mother usually won't let me go out on school nights, but this time she did on account of how it was the midterm exam. She was supposed to pick me up at ten, but Emily's father had to tell me what happened and drive me home."

"Why don't you rest, Bambi? I'll drive over to the cemetery and bring your mother back." I patted her on the arm and left before she could protest, if she intended to do so. She was more likely to be so relieved at my departure that she was unable to get out a single word.

I parked beside the stone wall girding the cemetery, stuck

my fists in my pockets, and walked up a path tangential to the canvas tent. I made an effort to keep my face lowered, although I doubted Michelle would recognize me—since we'd never met. I was not surprised to see two women seated on the grass, legs crossed, hands flickering as they talked. Nor was I surprised to hear laughter. After all, these were two old friends with a history that spanned twenty years. They'd shared stories of married life, of children, of financial woes, of vacations, of triumphs and disasters.

They froze when I veered at the last minute and stopped in front of them. "Charlie Kirkpatrick and Michelle McQueen?" I inquired politely, if rhetorically. "I'm Claire Malloy. I own the Book Depot, and my daughter, Caron, works on the school newspaper with Bambi."

I studied their faces; neither had the glint of a predatory woman incapable of female friendship. Michelle was pretty, if not beautiful, and there was a gap between her front teeth that indicated she was not obsessed with perfection. Charlie had cropped dark hair, a wide mouth, and a longish chin that reminded me of Luanne, especially when she was tired.

These women were tired, but I would be, too, if I'd been propping up a facade for six months, culminating in what amounted to premeditated murder.

"Why are you here?" asked Michelle.

"A better question," I said, gesturing at Charlie, "is why is she here? Isn't she the woman that took advantage of your friendship to have an affair with your husband and then run him down in the driveway?"

Charlie winced. "I came by after the funeral to try to explain what happened to Michelle. Having an affair with Ethan was the lowest, vilest thing I've ever done in my life. I'd been deeply depressed all winter, drinking too much and thinking too hard about how empty my life was. It's taken five years for the divorce to sink in, and once my son left for college and I had the house all to myself, I fell apart."

Michelle squeezed her friend's hand and said, "I knew you were unhappy when Chad left, but I had no idea how bad it was. Ethan must have sensed your vulnerability and moved in like a vulture, just like he did with his clients, such as that woman who was brutalized by her husband and the poor girl last year whose husband and baby were killed in a car wreck." She grimaced. "I'm sure there were others, but I was naive, and he was adept at lying."

"And you were always the last to know," I said as I looked down at her watery eyes and white face. "I wish I believed it, but in this case, Ethan was the last to know, wasn't he?"

"To know what?" Charlie said, then exchanged a quick look with Michelle.

"To know he was having an affair with you," I said. "The plan is very good, by the way. Two old friends stop seeing each other when one suspects the other of the affair. The husband purportedly breaks it off, and the mistress storms the house in a drunken rage and manages to kill him in the ensuing scene. Why, with the wife to testify, the mistress might get off with only a few months in the county jail—or even working weekends in a crisis center or a nursing home. In the meantime, the grieving widow collects the insurance money and bravely faces the future with a daughter who'll be away at college in a year. What were you two planning to do?"

"Buy a bed-and-breakfast," Charlie admitted in a low voice. "The one we stayed at in Eureka Springs is on the market."

"And travel during the off season," added Michelle. "Ethan refused to go anywhere that didn't have at least one championship golf course, which ruled out most of the planet. Charlie found a great deal on a two-week trip to

France, but Ethan wouldn't even open the brochure. I was so excited about bicycling and hot-air ballooning through the chateau country, and all he did was shake his head and mention that damned resort on Hilo we've been to every year for the last decade."

I sighed. "I don't know what will happen now. I'll have to tell the police what I know, but it's up to them to prove it."

Michelle smiled serenely. "There's a paper trail of motel receipts, dinners for two on nights when I was visiting his mother, long-distance calls to Charlie, credit card invoices for expensive gifts that never made it home."

"I've been seeing a psychiatrist," Charlie contributed, "and I was so overwhelmed with guilt that I had to tell him about the affair. He's been very worried about my rages and occasional suicide attempts. In the last few months, his service has logged quite a few hysterical midnight calls."

Michelle rolled her eyes. "You'll never get those bloodstains out of the bedspread, dummy. You're dying to get the sofa recovered, but you have to slit your wrists in bed."

"I am so confused," Charlie said, then started to laugh.

Michelle leaned against her, her laughter lilting despite the proximity of her freshly planted husband, and looked up at me with a grin. "Please forgive me—it must be the shock. But if you could see this hideous mauve sofa . . ."

I turned away and took several steps, then looked back at them. "A friend in need, huh?"

They were already lost in a conversation of bicycles and passports. I walked back to my car and drove home, imagining a scenario in which Luanne would risk a jail sentence, albeit a short one, to murder an inconvenient husband in exchange for a trip to France. It was easier than I'd anticipated. I refused to allow myself to ponder the inverse position.

When I arrived home, I went to Caron's door and was about to knock when I heard her say, "I can't tell you my source, Louis, but I swear on last year's *Falcon Crier* that Rhonda has a date with Bruce this Friday while you're at the Southside game. All you have to do is call her the next morning and ask her why she was seen at the drive-in movie with him, and why the car windows were steamier than a sauna." There was a pause. "I can't tell you, but my source is very, very good. We just thought you'd be interested, that's all. I've got to work on this really mindless algebra assignment, so 'bye!"

As I lowered my hand, I heard Inez's muted laugh. It was nearly drowned out by Caron's cackles of victory. Shrugging, I went to the kitchen to fix a drink, then got comfortable on the sofa and reached for the telephone. I should have called Peter to tell him what I'd learned, but I found myself automatically dialing Luanne's number. After all, a good friend deserves to be the first to know.

Maggody Files: D.W.I.

Thursdays aren't the busiest days for outbursts of criminal activity in Maggody, Arkansas (pop. 755). Neither are Sundays, Mondays, Tuesdays, and Wednesdays. Long about Friday, things pick up in anticipation of the weekend, although when we're talking grand theft auto, it means some teenager took off in his pa's pickup. A hit-and-run has to do with a baseball and a broken window at the Pot o' Gold trailer park. The perpetrator of larceny tends to be a harried mother who forgot to pay for gas at the convenience store, most likely because one of the toddlers in the back seat of the station wagon chose that moment to vomit copiously into the front seat.

I say all this with authority, because I, Ariel Hanks, am the chief of police, and it's my sworn duty to drag the errant driver home by his ear, and send the batter over to mumble a confession and offer to make reparation. Why, I've been known to go all the way out to Joyce Lambertino's house to have a diet soda and a slice of pound cake, admire her counted cross-stitch, and take her money to the Kwik-Stoppe-Shoppe. And bring her back the change.

Other than that, I occasionally run a speed trap out by the skeletal remains of Purtle's Esso Station, where there's a nice patch of shade and some incurious cows. I swap dirty jokes with the sheriff's deputies when they drop by for coffee. Every now and then I wander around Cotter's Ridge, on the very obscure chance I might stumble across Raz Buchanon's moonshine still. It's up there somewhere, along with ticks, chiggers, mosquitoes, brambles, and nasty-tempered copperheads.

The rest of the time I devote to napping, reading, wondering why I'm back in Maggody, and doing whatever's necessary to eat three meals a day at Ruby Bee's Bar & Grill. The proprietor (a.k.a. my mother) is a worthy opponent, despite her chubby body and twinkly eyes. She's adjusted to having her daughter do what she considers a man's job, and she's resigned to my divorce and my avowed devotion to the single life. This is not to say I don't hear about my failings on a regular basis, both from her and her spindly, red-haired cohort, Estelle Oppers, who runs a beauty shop in her living room— and is as eager as Ruby Bee is to run my life. But I don't believe in running; there's nothing wrong with a nice, easy walk (except on Cotter's Ridge, and that's already been mentioned).

But the particular Thursday under discussion turned ugly. I was at the PD, yanking open desk drawers to watch the roaches scurry for cover. When the telephone rang, I reluctantly shut the drawer and picked up the receiver.

"Sheriff Dorfer says to meet him by the creek out on County 103," the dispatcher said with her customary charm. "Right now."

"Shall I bring a bucket of bait and a six-pack?"

"Just git yourself over there, Arly. Sheriff Dorfer's at the scene, and he ain't gonna be all that tickled if you show up acting like you thought it was a picnic."

It was not a picnic. I parked behind several official vehicles, settled my sunglasses, and slithered and slipped down a fresh path of destruction to the edge of Boone Creek. Harve Dorfer was talking to a man in a torn army jacket who was wiping blood from his face with a wadded handkerchief. A pair of grim deputies watched. Beyond them lay a lumpish form covered by a blanket. The rear half of a truck stuck out of the water as if poised in a dive.

"You're a real work of art," Harve growled, then stalked over to me, an unlit cigar butt wedged in the corner of his mouth. He aimed a finger at me, but turned and looked at his deputies. "Les, you and John Earl take this stinkin' drunk up to the road and have the medics check him. If nothing's broke, take him to the office and book him. If something is, go along with him and wait at the emergency room until he's patched up. Then take him to the office and throw the whole dadgum book at him."

I studied the object of Harve's displeasure. Red Gromwell was local, a young guy, maybe thirty, with a sly face already turning soft and greasy hair the color of a rotting orange. At the moment, he had a swollen lip, the beginnings of a black eye, and a ragged streak of blood down the side of his face. His knuckles were raw. His jacket was stained with blood, as were the baggy jeans that rode low on his hips out of deference to his beer gut. He gave me a foolish grin, dropped the handkerchief, and crumpled to the ground. The deputies hauled him to his feet, and the three began to climb toward the road.

"Drunker than a boiled owl," Harve said, firing up the cigar butt. "Says he and a guy named Buell Fumitory was out riding around, sharing a bottle and yucking it up. All of a sudden the truck's bouncing down the hill like one of those bumper cars at the county fair. Says he was thrown out the window and landed way yonder in that clump of brush. Buell over there wasn't as lucky."

I folded my arms and tried to be a cool, detached cop. My eyes kept sneaking to the shrouded body on the ground, however, and I doubt Harve was fooled one whit. I tried to swallow, but my mouth was as dry as the dusty road behind us. "Did Buell drown?" I asked.

"I can't say right offhand. He was banged up pretty bad from hitting his face against the steering wheel who knows how many times. It doesn't much matter—in particular to him. Red said by the time he could git himself up and stagger to the edge of the water, it was clear there wasn't anything to do for Buell. He did manage to climb back to the road and flag down a truck driver who called us."

"Red's not the heroic sort," I said, shaking my head. "He'd just as soon run down a dog as bother to brake."

"You know him?"

"Yes indeed. He works at the body shop and brawls at the pool hall. I had some unpleasant encounters with him after his wife finally got fed up with him and filed for divorce. Twice I drove her to the women's shelter in Farberville and urged her to stay for a few days, but she scooted right back and refused to file charges, so there wasn't much I could do."

"One of those, huh?" Harve said through a cloud of noxious cigar smoke.

"One of those." I again found myself staring at the blanket. "Buell Fumitory kept to himself, so I don't know much about him. He moved here . . . oh, a year ago, and worked at the supermarket. He came into Ruby Bee's every now and then for a beer. He seemed okay to me."

"According to this Red fellow, Buell was driving at the time of the accident. I reckon it's too late to give him a ticket." Harve snuffed out the cigar butt and looked over my shoulder. "Here come the boys with the body bag. Tell ya what, Arly," he said, putting his arm around me and escorting me up the hill, "I'm gonna let you have this one for your very own. I need Les and John Earl to finish up the paperwork on those burglaries over in Hasty, and I myself am gonna be busier than a stump-tailed cow in fly time with office chores."

I shrugged off his arm. "Like posing for the media with the latest haul of marijuana? This sudden activity doesn't have anything to do with the upcoming election, does it?"

"You just hunt up the next of kin and write me a couple of pages of official blather," he said. Trying not to smirk, he left me at the road and went down to supervise the medics.

As I stood there berating myself for getting stuck so easily with nothing but tedious paperwork, a tow truck came down the road. Once the body and the truck were removed, the squirrels would venture back, as would the birds, the bugs, and the fish that lurked in the muddy creek. The splintered saplings would be replaced by a new crop. Three months from then, I told myself with a grimace, there would be nothing left to remind folks about the dangers of D.W.I. In some states, it's called other things. In Arkansas, we opt for the simple and descriptive Driving While Intoxicated. Might as well call it Dying While Intoxicated.

"It doesn't make a plugged nickel's worth of sense," Ruby Bee proclaimed from behind the bar. She rinsed off the glasses in the sink, wiped her hands on her apron, and gazed beadily at Estelle, who was drinking a beer and gobbling up pretzels like she was a paying customer.

"That sort of thing happens all the time," Estelle countered. "They were drunk, and anybody with a smidgen of the sense God gave a goose knows it's asking for trouble to go drinking and driving, particularly out on those twisty back roads. Remember that time I was coming back from a baby shower in Emmet, and this big ol' deer came scampering into the road, and I nearly—"

"Nobody said there was a deer involved. Lottie said that Elsie happened to hear Red talking to some fellow at the launderette earlier this morning, and he said Buell was singing and howling like a tomcat and was a sight too far gone to keep his eyes or anything else on the road." She began to dry the glasses on a dishrag, all the while frowning and trying to figure out what was nagging at her. "The thing is," she added slowly, "I didn't think Buell was like that. He was always real nice when he worked in produce. One time I bought a watermelon, and when I cut—"

"I don't see why he couldn't have been real nice and also been willing to drink cheap whisky and take a drive."

"I ain't saying he wasn't," Ruby Bee said, still speaking slowly and getting more bumfuzzled by the minute. "But I'll tell you one thing, Estelle—he never came in here and guzzled down a couple of pitchers like Red did. Like Red did before I threw him out on his skinny behind, that is. It like to cost me three hundred dollars to get the jukebox fixed. And to think he busted it just because his ex-wife was drinking a glass of beer with that tire salesman!"

"He was hotter than a fire in a pepper mill, wasn't he?" Estelle said as she picked up a pretzel. "I wish somebody'd find the gumption to mention to him that what his ex-wife does is none of his business. It ain't like he bought a wife; he was only renting one. It's a crying shame he wasn't the one to end up in the creek so Gayle can get on with her life and stop having to peek over her shoulder every time she steps out of the house."

"How'd she take the news?"

Estelle lowered her voice, although anybody could see there wasn't another soul in the barroom, much less hanging over her shoulder like a lapel. "Well, Lottie said Mrs. Jim Bob happened to run by Gayle's with some ironing, and Gayle wouldn't even come to the door. Mrs. Jim Bob saw the curtain twitch, so she knew perfectly well that Gayle was home at the time."

"I don't see that she has any reason to . . ."

Estelle gave her a pitying look. "To avoid Mrs. Jim Bob? I'd say we all had darn good reasons to do that. I could make you a list as long as your arm."

"Unless, of course . . ."

"Unless what?"

"Well, if Gayle was . . ."

"I do believe you could finish a sentence, Mrs. Dribble Mouth, and do it before the sun sets in Bogart County."

Not bothering to respond, Ruby Bee stared at the jukebox with a deepening frown. "You know," she said about the time Estelle was preparing to make another remark, "the last time I saw Gayle at the Emporium, she was looking right frumpy. What she needs is a perm, Estelle, and you're the one to give it to her. I suspect it'll have to be for free; she barely makes minimum wage at the poultry plant in Starley City. Why doncha call her right now and make an appointment?"

"For free?" Estelle gasped. "Why in tarnation would I do a thing like that?"

Ruby Bee curled her finger, and this time she was the one to speak in a low, conspiratorial voice. Estelle managed not to butt in, and ten minutes later she was dialing Gayle Gromwell's telephone number.

The next morning I got the address of Buell Fumitory's rent house from the manager at the supermarket. He told me that Buell had worked there for most of a year, caused no trouble, took no unauthorized days off, and got along with the other employees.

Armed with the above piercing insights, I drove out past Raz Buchanon's shack to an ordinary frame house in a scruffy yard. A rusty subcompact was parked beside the house, but no one answered my repeated knocks. I considered doing something clever with a skeleton key or a credit card to gain entry. However, having neither, I opened the front door and went inside.

The interior was as ordinary as the exterior. It was clearly a bachelor's domain. There were a few dirty ashtrays and a beer can on the coffee table, odds and ends of food in the refrigerator, chipped dishes and a cracked cup in the cabinets. The only anomaly was a vase with a handful of wilted daisies, but even tomato stackers can have a romantic streak.

I continued on my merry way. The bedroom was small and cluttered, but no more so than my apartment usually was. The closet contained basic clothing and fishing equipment. The drawer in the bedside table had gum wrappers, nail clippers, a long overdue electric bill, and an impressive selection of condom packets. Perhaps somebody in the morgue would encourage Buell to continue practicing safe sex in the netherworld.

In the distance, most likely at Raz's place, a dog began to bark dispiritedly. As if in response, the house creaked and sighed. It wasn't a mausoleum, and I wasn't about to lapse into a gothic thing involving involuntary shivers and a compulsion to clutch my bosom and flutter my eyelashes. On the other hand, I recalled the blanketed body alongside the creek, and I wasted no time, pawing through dresser drawers until I found a stack of letters and an address book.

I sat down on the bed and flipped through the latter until I found the listing for Aunt Pearl in Boise. If she was not the official next of kin, she would know who was. The letters turned out to be commercial greeting cards, all signed with a smiley face. I made a frowny face, stuffed them back in the drawer, and returned to the PD to see if Aunt Pearl might be sitting by her telephone in Boise.

She was, but she was also hard of hearing and very old. Once I'd conveyed the news, she admitted she was the only living relative. Her financial situation precluded funeral arrangements. I assured her that we would deal with it, hung up, and leaned back in my chair to ponder how best to share this with Harve. There was very little of value at Buell's house. A small television, furniture that would go to the Salvation Army (if they'd take it), and a couple of boxes of personal effects. The pitiful car would bring no more than a hundred dollars.

The pitiful car. I propped my feet on the corner of the desk and tried to figure out why there was a car, pitiful or not, parked at Buell's house. He did not seem like a two-car family. Glumly noting that the water stain on the ceiling had expanded since last I'd studied it, I called the manager at the supermarket and asked him what Buell had driven. He grumbled but agreed to ask the employees, and came back with a description of the subcompact.

Red Gromwell drove an ancient Mustang; I'd pulled him over so many times that I knew the license plate by heart. The pickup truck in the creek had been gray, or white and dirty. I thought this over for a while (bear in mind it was Friday morning, so I wasn't preparing to foil bank robberies or negotiate with kidnappers).

I called the sheriff's department and got Harve on the line.

"You're not backing out on that D.W.I. report, are you?" he asked before I could get out a word. "I hate to stick you with it, Arly, but I'm up to my neck in some tricky figures for the upcoming quorum meeting, and one of the county judges says—"

"What'd you do with Red Gromwell?"

There was a lengthy silence. At last Harve exhaled and said, "Nothing much, damn it. We kept him in the drunk tank for twelve hours. This morning he called his cousin for bail money and strolled out like a preacher on his way to count the offering. I checked with the county prosecutor, but it ain't worth bothering with. If he'd been driving, we could cause him some grief. Not that much, though. Get his driver's license suspended, slap him with a fat fine. The judge'd lecture him for twenty minutes, and maybe give him some probation. The prisons are stuffed to the gills right now, and I sure don't need to offer the likes of Red Gromwell room and board, courtesy of Stump County."

I waited until he stopped sighing, then asked him to ascertain the ownership of the truck that had been pulled out of Boone Creek. He huffed and puffed some more while I wondered how badly the PD roof was leaking and finally agreed to have Les call the tow shop (sigh), get the truck's plate number (siigh), and call the state office (siiigh) to see who all was named on the registration.

On that breezy note, we parted. I did some noisy exhaling of my own, but all it accomplished was to make me woozy. It occurred to me that I was in need of both local gossip and a blue plate special, so I abandoned any pretense of diligent detection and walked down the road to Ruby Bee's Bar & Grill, the hot spot for food and fiction.

It was closed. Irritated, I went back to my car, drove to the Dairee Dee-Lishus where the food was less palatable but decidedly better than nothing, and promised myself a quiet picnic out by the rubble of the gas station. Twenty minutes later, I was turning down County 103.

"It'd be cute all curly around your face," Ruby Bee said brightly. "Brush those bangs out of your eyes and wear a little

175

makeup, and you'd look just like a homecoming queen."

"I don't know," Gayle Gromwell said. She didn't sound like she did, either. She sounded more like she was real sorry about coming to Estelle's Hair Fantasies, even if the perm was free. Nobody'd said the event was open to the public.

Estelle nudged Ruby Bee out of the way. "I happen to be professionally trained in these matters," she said with a pinched frown. "Now, Gayle honey, I have to agree that those bangs make you look like a dog that came out of the rain a day late. I'm just going to snip a bit here and there, give you some nice, soft curls, and then we'll see if maybe you don't want an auburn rinse."

Gayle looked a little pouty, but this wasn't surprising since she wasn't much older than twenty and still had a few blemishes and the faint vestiges of baby fat. She slouched in the chair and gazed blackly at her image in the mirror, refusing to meet Estelle's inquisitive eyes or even Ruby Bee's penetrating stare. "Oh, go ahead and do whatever you want. I know my hair looks awful, but I don't care. Why don't you shave it off?"

"It's going be real pretty," Estelle said nervously. This wasn't what she and Ruby Bee had hoped for, although Gayle had come and that was the first hurdle. She wiggled her eyebrows at Ruby Bee. "Don't you think Gayle here will have every boy in town chasing after her?"

Ruby Bee knew a cue when she heard one. "I just hope Red's simmered down. Remember when he put his fist through the jukebox because of that tire salesman? They charged me three hundred dollars."

They both looked at Gayle, wondering what she'd say. Her eyes were closed, but as they watched, a tear squeezed out and slunk down her cheek alongside her nose. Within the hour, they had the whole teary, hiccuppy, disjointed story.

★ ★ ★ ★ ★

"Two weeks ago?" I echoed, admittedly less than brilliantly. "The truck was purchased two weeks ago?"

"A private sale," Les continued. "I tracked down the previous owner, who said he'd advertised the damn thing for three weeks running and was about to sell it for scrap when some guy showed up with a hundred bucks."

"Some guy? What did he look like?"

"Nothing special. Dark hair, wearing jeans and a work shirt, sunglasses, cap. Average height and weight, no initials carved in his forehead or neon antlers or anything."

"And he didn't catch the guy's name, I suppose?"

"You suppose right. This was strictly cash-and-carry."

I tried once more. "What about the registration papers?"

"Never transferred."

I hung up and went to the back room of the PD to glower at my evidence. It didn't take long. The bloodstained handkerchief was in one plastic bag and an empty liter whisky bottle in another. I hadn't been in the mood to take scrapings of mud from the bank or water from the creek. Harve, the deputies, the medics, and the tow truck operator had all tromped around; if there had been a telltale footprint, it had been obliterated (and I couldn't imagine a footprint telling much of a tale, anyway).

There was no point in dusting the bottle for fingerprints. If I bothered, and then found Red and took his to compare, I'd have a lovely match. It was a policeish activity, but also a futile one. As for the handkerchief, I knew where the blood came from and I didn't care where the handkerchief did.

And I knew where the truck came from, but I didn't know who had bought it or why. I realized I again was making a frowny face. This was of no significance, but it led my thoughts back to the smiley faces on the cards, and that led me to the contents of the bedside drawer, the daisies, the white pickup truck, and before too long I was staring at the whisky bottle and wondering how I could prove Red Gromwell had murdered Buell Fumitory—soberly and in cold blood. Then I realized I had the evidence in front of me. I went back to the telephone, called Les, and said, "Do you have a date tonight?"

"I don't think my wife will approve, but what do you have in mind?"

"What happened to Gayle's hair?" I said to Ruby Bee as I watched Gayle and Les settle in a back booth. "Didn't her mother warn her about sticking a fork in a socket?"

Ruby Bee leaned across the bar and whispered, "This ain't the time for smart remarks. I don't seem to recollect anyone complimenting you on that schoolmarm hair of yours. I happen to have something that you might find interestin', if you can shut your mouth long enough to hear it."

I meekly shut my mouth, mostly because I might have time to eat a piece of pie before the fireworks started. Before I could hear the big news, Estelle perched on the bar stool next to me, craned her head around until she spotted Gayle, and then turned back with a self-righteous smile. "I just knew that auburn rinse would be perfect. If Arly here would let me re-style her hair, she'd look just as nice as Gayle."

"So that's why I had to eat at the Dee-Lishus today," I said accusingly. I resisted the urge to run my fingers through my hair, which would have undone my bun and left me vulnerable to further cosmetological attacks. "Just once I wish you two would stay off the case. Believe it or not, I am more than capable of—"

"Gayle was having an affair with Buell," Ruby Bee said.

I did not relent. "I figured as much, and I did it all by myself. I did not require the assistance of two overgrown Nancy Drews to—"

"And Red found out," Estelle said. "Last week he busted in on 'em and made all kinds of nasty threats. I find that a mite suspicious, considering what happened last evening." She blinked at Ruby Bee, not blankly but frostily. "If Arly already knew about Gayle and Buell, why did I end up doing her perm for free?"

Ruby Bee retreated until she bumped into the beer tap. "Arly doesn't know everything. Just ask her if she knows that Buell didn't like to go carousing like some, and hardly ever got drunk on account of the medication he took for a recurring bladder problem. And wouldn't have gone riding around with Red if his life depended on it."

"Don't ask me anything," I rumbled. I was about to elaborate on my irritation when I spotted Red coming across the dance floor. He still looked a bit battered, the black eye having blossomed and the swollen lip giving him a petulant sneer. He was not wearing bloodstained clothing, however, and he moved easily for someone reputedly thrown fifty feet from a careening vehicle.

He froze in the middle of the floor, ignoring the couples cruising around him. His fingers curled into fists, and a muscle in his neck bulged like a piece of rope. Clearly, the first of the bottle rockets was lit. I slid off the stool and caught up with him as he reached the booth where Gayle and Les were sitting.

"What the hell did you do to your hair?" he asked Gayle. When she shrugged, he jabbed his thumb at Les.

"Who's this?"

She looked up defiantly. "None of your business, Red. We've been divorced for two years now, and you ain't got any right to act like a crybaby if I go out with someone."

"I didn't act like a crybaby when I caught you in bed with that wimp from the supermarket, did I?" he said, looming over her. "Guess you won't be romping with him any more, unless you aim to crawl in the casket with him."

Les put down his beer. "Now, wait just a minute, buddy. This woman doesn't have to take that kind of talk from—"

"Shut up or I'll shove that glass down your throat," Red snarled. "Now, listen up, Gayle Gromwell. You git yourself out of that booth and on your way home afore I drag this mama's boy outside to rearrange his pretty little face."

"You can't tell me what to do," she said sulkily.

Red pulled back his hand to slap her, but I grabbed his arm and hung on until he relaxed. "Gayle's right, Red—you can't tell her what to do," I said. "She's a single woman, and she's allowed to date whomever she chooses. In this case, she's chosen to date a deputy sheriff, which means you're threatening an officer of the law. In front of an entire roomful of witnesses, too."

He realized all the customers were watching and, from their expressions, enjoying the scene. Ruby Bee thoughtfully had unplugged the jukebox so nobody would miss a word.

"Okay," he muttered to me, then stared at Gayle. "You keep in mind what I said to you the other night, you hear?"

I tapped him on the shoulder. "Was this when you invited your old pal Buell to share a bottle of whisky and enjoy the moonlight?"

"Naw, that was yesterday after work. I went by his house to tell him I was wrong to bust down the door like I did. I told him that sometimes I go kind of crazy when I think about Gayle with another man. He was right understanding, and pretty soon we decided to run into Farberville and get ourselves a bottle. We was talking about deer season when he lost control of the truck. You know what happened then."

"Yes, I do," I said, nodding. "Why was Buell driving the truck you bought in Little Rock two weeks ago? You paid good money for it, and I'm surprised you weren't driving."

The bruises under his eye stayed dark, but the rest of his face paled. "I dunno. I thought he was soberer than me."

"It's a good thing you weren't in the Mustang, isn't it?" I continued, still pretending we were having a polite conversation. "I know you're awfully fond of it."

"Helluva car," he said.

"Which is why you bought the truck. You weren't about to total your Mustang that way. I checked around town today, and nobody saw you and Buell driving down the road in the white pickup." I crossed my fingers. "But Raz saw you drive by his place in the Mustang late afternoon, and come back by. He didn't see Buell then, but I guess he'd need X-ray vision to see a body in the trunk, wouldn't he?"

"What are you saying?" Gayle said, gulping. "Did he kill Buell?"

"I already told the sheriff all about it," Red muttered.

I shook my head. "You told the sheriff a stale old fairy tale, Red. You went to Buell's and beat him up, put him in the trunk, and drove to your place to switch vehicles. Then you collected the whisky, went out to the hill on County 103, and sent Buell down the hill and into the creek. He was unconscious, so he didn't have much of a chance to get out of the truck."

He gave me a frightened look. "You got any proof, cop lady?"

"You drained the bottle after the wreck, so we'd figure you were drunk. I found it in the woods. If you had it with you in the truck, then you and it went flying out the window together. Why didn't it break?"

"That doesn't prove anything."

"You'd better hope Buell's fingerprints are on it," I said, "and that the alcohol level in his blood indicates he was drunk." I waited politely, but he didn't seem to have much to say. "Oh, yes, and there's one more thing, Red. You'd better start praying the blood on that handkerchief matches your type and doesn't have any traces of the medication Buell was taking."

"Medication?" Red said, sounding as if he were in need of some at the moment. He didn't improve when Les stood up, recited the Miranda warning, and cuffed him.

Once they were gone, I glowered at Ruby Bee until she headed for the jukebox, then sat down across from Gayle. "Red'll be out on bail by Monday. I suggest you spend the weekend thinking about why you're willing to play the role of victim. Get some counseling at the women's shelter if it'll help, and change the lock on your front door."

Her smile was dreamy. "Who'd have thought Red would actually kill somebody over me?"

"One of these days he'll kill you," I said, then left her to her pathetic fantasies and went back to the PD to brood.

During the course of the weekend, I'd be obliged to run in some drunks, bust a couple of minors in possession, and intervene in domestic disputes. With luck, we'd all survive, and on Monday morning, bright and early, I'd grab my radar gun and a good book, and head for that patch of shade . . . unless I decided to take a hike on Cotter's Ridge. You just never know where crime will erupt in Maggody, Arkansas (pop. 755).

The Maggody Files: Death in Bloom

"The thing is," Ruby Bee announced before Estelle could once again start in squawking like a blue jay, which, for the record, she'd been doing for the last ten minutes, give or take, "Beryl makes superior apple pies. I'm thinking she might be inclined to share her secret. That's why we're doing this."

Estelle adjusted the rearview mirror and made sure her beehive of red hair was securely pinned and ready to withstand anything short of hurricane-strength winds. "I still don't see why the both of us should close up shop and go over to drink coffee, eat a piece of pie, and be so bored we're gonna wish we'd joined a book club. Beryl's pies take the blue ribbon every year at the county fair. That doesn't mean I want to spend an hour admiring her begonias and zucchinis."

Ruby Bee sighed as she drove up County 103. "Did you hear what I said, Estelle? Beryl's apple pies have a certain something. I've been trying to figure out for most of thirty years what her secret is. Times I think it's an extra dash of nutmeg or cinnamon, and then I think it must be ginger. I realize this sounds odd, but there are nights I toss and turn until dawn."

"Odd," Estelle echoed in a voice meant to irritate Ruby Bee, which it most certainly did. "You're saying you can't sleep on account of Beryl Blanchard winning the blue ribbon at the county fair every year on account of ginger? I spend a lot more hours worrying if the IRS will come after me—or if a slobbering serial killer will bust into my house."

Ruby Bee turned up the gravel driveway to Beryl's house. "I suspect you're losing sleep over something less likely than Idalupino Buchanon's face appearing on the cover of *People* magazine. We're gonna have pie and coffee, spend a few minutes with Buck, and dutifully admire the garden. If Beryl wants to give me her secret recipe, so be it. If not, no one has yet dared to criticize the apple pie I serve at the bar and grill."

"Not if they want to live to see the dawning of another day," Estelle muttered, then looked at the weedy pasture as Ruby Bee's car bounced up the rutted driveway. The house was, at best, serviceable. The garden, on the other hand, was enough to suck the breath out of any soul's body. Yellows and reds and fuchsias and oranges and pinks and purples—every glorious color on the spectrum—exploded from all sides. Blooms stretched to meet the sun; others cascaded like iridescent waterfalls.

"You got to admit," Ruby Bee said solemnly, "that this is something. Beryl may not be on the top of my list of favorite people, but you'd almost think she gets seed catalogs direct from the Garden of Eden."

"Then we'd better keep an eye out for the serpent," Estelle said as she unbuckled her seat belt.

Ruby Bee frowned but held her peace as they got out of the car. Maggody was a quiet little town most of the time, although things seemed to keep happening. Today, however, held no undertones of menace. Arly, who just happened to be the chief of police as well as Ruby Bee's daughter, had last been seen napping at her desk at the two-room police department, most likely dreaming of an escape to a somewhat more invigorating lifestyle that precluded moonshiners and dim-witted locals. There were no banks in Maggody, so the odds of a robbery-in-progress were limited. Anyone who imprudently ran the sole stoplight was in luck for the next hour or so.

"Ruby Bee, Estelle!" shrieked Beryl as she arose from a bed of exceedingly tall purple perennials. "I am delighted that you came! This is such a treat for me. So few people drop by these days. Buck and Sylvie are as excited as I am."

Ruby Bee pasted on a smile. "You know I'm always in the mood for pie and coffee. How's Buck doing?"

Beryl, whose gray hair held a tint of the same purple as the flowers surrounding her, wiped her face on her shirt cuff, leaving a smudge of dirt on her otherwise properly school-marmish features. "The wheelchair's not been easy for him, but he knows he has to be careful. He gets all these crazy ideas about European tours and African safaris and how we can travel to all these places like he never had the heart surgery. Sylvie's forever bringing home brochures about cruises and the like. Silliness! You name another place on earth more beautiful than where we're standing." She spread her arms as if embracing nature in its entirety. "What more could anyone want?"

"Something more exciting than Maggody," Buck said as he wheeled onto the porch. "I just want to go while we can. A few years from now, maybe I'll be content to sit here, watching the turkey vultures circle in on me. I was in the United States Navy, as you ladies must know. We had shore leave in Athens and Naples and a whole lot of fascinating places. I keep trying to persuade Beryl here to take a gander at them while we can. I drank a little ouzo in my time, I did, and climbed to the very rim of Vesuvius. One night when I was on the Isle of Capri—"

"We don't have any reason to travel," Beryl cut in. "We've got a vegetable garden, an orchard ripe with peaches and apples, and flowers that could dazzle a blind man. Why would I want to go to some foreign place where I'm likely to get a disease? Home is where you get meat loaf, mashed potatoes, and apple pie."

Buck made a gesture that indicated he'd heard the argument more times than he could count. "Just thought I'd mention it," he said darkly as he spun around and went inside.

"He doing okay otherwise?" asked Ruby Bee.

Beryl shrugged as she picked up a muddy trowel and stacked together several empty plastic pots. "He'd do better if he did away with all his foolish ideas about traveling. Taking care of the property is a full-time job, what with planting in the spring, tending in the summer, harvesting in the fall, and pruning and planning in the winter. It's not like Sylvie could step in for even a week or two. I'd be terrified that she'd make such a mess of everything that it'd take me two or three years to recover."

"I just love your hollyhocks," Estelle said tactfully.

"Me, too," Beryl said. "Now let's go inside for pie and coffee, and then we'll have a nice stroll. I'm particularly pleased with the dianthus along the back fence. It has a wonderful cinnamon scent."

Ruby Bee smiled with all the subtlety of a fox teetering on the henhouse roof. "Speakin' of cinnamon, Beryl . . ."

They went into the house. The living room was dark and sparse, what with the drapes drawn and the wood floor unadorned. The obligatory crocheted doilies were spread across the arms of the sofa. Photographs of dyspeptic ancestors glowered from the walls. Tables that might have held vases of nature's glories were bare, with the exception of the odd crystal dish that most likely had arrived as a wedding present and had never since held so much as a mint. The only book in sight was a family Bible.

"Sylvie!" Beryl called as they went down the hall. "We have company. I hope you're not sulking in your room." She lowered her voice and looked back at Ruby Bee and Estelle. "Sylvie's not always fit for company. She did insist on baking the apple pie this morning, though."

The baker under discussion trudged into the kitchen. She was thick, pale, somewhat sallow, and clearly unhappy. "You didn't mention company, Ma."

Ruby Bee managed a smile. "And how are you doing these days, Sylvie? Still attending the community college in Farberville?"

"No," Sylvie muttered. "I did for a year, but now I'm here, taking care of things. Maybe down the road I can get some kind of degree." She put on an apron and began to shove pots and pans into the gray dishwasher in the sink. "How's Arly doing?"

"Real fine," Ruby Bee said, looking at Estelle for help. A bullfrog caught in a spotlight might have appeared less panicky.

"Yeah, real fine," said Estelle. "Why, Arly's just as happy as a hog in a wallow. I'm sure she'd like to be out and about with men of an acceptable persuasion, but she's willing to settle for a grilled cheese sandwich and happy hour at the bar and grill. How about you, Sylvie? You ever think about coming by for a beer? Things start jumping on Friday afternoons."

Rather than responding, Sylvie grimly set a pie on the dinette. "Coffee'll be ready in a minute," she said, then disappeared down the hallway.

Beryl sighed. "I just don't know what to do with that girl. I've made it clear she can take a class or two at the community college, as long as she can work around Buck's needs. I'm just not strong enough to deal with him. I can't help him in or out of his chair, or see to his basic needs in certain matters. I want you to know I've tried, Ruby Bee and Estelle; the spirit is willing, but . . ."

"How about I pour the coffee?" Ruby Bee said. She waited until Beryl nodded, then found cups and saucers in a cabinet and filled each cup. "Shall I cut the pie?"

Beryl sighed. "These days, the complaints are enough to wear me out. Sylvie acts like we should find a way to pay a private nurse to see to Buck, but we can't. He spends his days whining about trips to foreign places. He needs the wheelchair, for pity's sake. I can't see myself lugging it up the gangplank of a ship or through the streets of some nasty place like Rome. I've been told that men"—her voice dropped to a whisper—"urinate in the streets. Can you imagine?"

"What about a cruise?" said Estelle as she accepted a plate from Ruby Bee. "Seems like there'd be one that caters to folks with disabilities. If Sylvie went along, you could visit some exotic ports and Buck might feel better."

"Some of the brochures say they do," Beryl said, "but most likely all they offer is wide bathroom doors. Besides, who'd look after my hybrid tea roses and prune the flowering crab apples? My garden means everything to me. I can't leave it to amateurs."

Ruby Bee was trying to come up with a rebuttal as she took a bite of the blue-ribbon pie. It was not easy to swallow. "A bit tart," she mumbled.

"I'd say so!" Beryl banged down her fork. "Sylvie! You march yourself in here right now, young lady. Here I invited guests for a nice dessert! This pie could pucker a face inside out. I'm so embarrassed I could just crawl under the table. I would never have served this if . . ."

Sylvie came into the kitchen. "Sorry, Mother. We ran out of sugar, and I thought I could adjust the recipe with honey. We've got some oatmeal cookies in the freezer. Maybe I can—"

Beryl rose with the menace of a summer squall. "That's quite enough, Sylvie. Give your father his bath, then remain in your room until I call for you."

"Now, Beryl," said Estelle, "it isn't like this was submitted to the committee at the county fair. All of us have substituted ingredients on occasion, although I can tell you molasses and Karo syrup just don't—"

"Shall we go outside?" Beryl said coldly.

Ruby Bee could tell it was not the moment to broach the most delicate topic of ginger versus an extra pinch of cinnamon. "It isn't that bad," she said to Sylvie, who was hovering in the doorway with a very peculiar look on her face. "The crust is very flaky and light, and nicely browned. Sometimes, mine are so soggy I feel like I plucked 'em out of a swamp."

Sylvie stared at her mother. "If I'd known we were expecting company, I would have tried more honey."

"Be sure to give your father's back a good scrub," Beryl said. She went across the kitchen, picked up a plastic bottle, and squirted cream into her palm. "I never go outside without a good slathering of sunscreen. We can't be too careful about skin cancer, can we?" Without waiting for a response, she began to apply it to her face, neck, and bare forearms.

Ruby Bee gave Estelle a hard look, then said, "We can't stay for long, Beryl. I'm supposed to be open for lunch, and I believe Estelle has an appointment before too long."

"That's right," Estelle said brightly. "Elsie McMay gets mighty testy if I keep her waiting for so much as a butterfly's flitter. We'll just take a quick gander at your garden and be on our way."

Beryl finished rubbing the lotion onto her skin. "Sylvie, you get busy with your duties. Tell your father I'll be in to see to his lunch after I've cut back the verbena. There are times when it feels like I'm the only person in this family able to take responsibility. You might as well have made that pie with green persimmons."

Ruby Bee gazed longingly at her car as they went outside. In a few minutes, she assured herself, she and Estelle could bounce down the driveway and turn on County 103. Not even the most delectable apple pie this side of heaven could warrant putting up with Beryl Blanchard and her mean-spirited tongue. The pie might have needed more honey, but Beryl needed an infusion.

Buck was seated in his wheelchair on the far corner of the porch. "Leaving so soon?" he called.

Ruby Bee sat down on a wicker chair beside him. "I was thinking how much I'd like to hear about your adventures in Naples and Athens," she said, wishing she had the gumption to grab his hand but keenly aware of Beryl's glare. "I'll bet you have all sorts of souvenirs and trinkets from your Navy days. Would you mind if I came by at another time?"

"If it works out," said Buck. "I may be gone."

She couldn't stop herself from clasping his bony arm. "Now, Buck, it can't be that bad. Beryl's feeding you a healthy diet of fresh fruits and vegetables. You're as nice and pink as"—she waved vaguely at the yard—"those blossoms over by the gate. Once you get back your strength, why, you might just be arm-wrasslin' at the bar and grill come Friday night. I seem to recollect you were pretty darn good at it once upon a time."

Beryl loomed over them. "Before he got sick, there was a

lot of things he could do. Now all he's good for is sitting and complaining. Estelle's around back, looking at the dianthus. You want to see them?"

Sylvie came out of the front door. "There's something I should tell you, Ma."

"I don't want to hear one more word from you, young lady," said Beryl. "You just take your father in and see to him, then go to your room and read your Bible until I call you. See if you can find any recipes using milk and honey."

"I'm warning you—you should hear me out."

Beryl's cheeks turned red. "Maybe I'll hear you out of house and home if you don't obey me. If I find so much as a single travel brochure on the table when I come back inside, I'll pack your bags myself and throw them at the end of the driveway. As for your father, he can learn to wear diapers and suck soup through a straw. Do you understand?"

Sylvie grabbed the handles of Buck's wheelchair and took him into the house. Ruby Bee was too appalled to do more than follow Beryl down the steps to the yard.

Beryl stopped at a trellis covered with sweet-scented, creamy blossoms. "This is an antique variety of honeysuckle called Serotina that blooms all summer. In the fall, it will be laden with lovely red berries that draw in our feathered friends. We are all nature's guardians, are we not? As opposed as I am to disorganization, I allow the butterfly weed just beyond the fence to thrive in order to nurture our winged visitors."

Ruby Bee was steeling herself to make a remark about nurturing those a mite closer to home when she saw a yellow jacket light on Beryl's arm. "You got another friend," she said, pointing.

Beryl flicked it off. "They never bother me. Out here in the splendors of . . ." She stopped to flick off another one. "Why, I haven't been stung since . . ."

"Take it easy," advised Ruby Bee, backing away. "Don't slap at em."

Beryl was staring in horror as several more yellow jackets began to crawl up her arm. "I'm allergic to them. Up until three years ago, I didn't know I was, but then I got stung and had to be taken to the emergency room. Why are they doing this? Make them go away!" She gasped as one lit on her cheek. "Away!"

Ruby Bee had no idea what she was supposed to do. "Don't make any sudden moves. They're just—"

"What?" shrieked Beryl as several more alit.

Estelle came dashing around the corner. "What in tarnation's wrong?"

"She must have disturbed a nest," Ruby Bee said, still not willing to move in any closer. "All they're doing is investigating thus far. As long as she doesn't . . ."

Beryl began to slap at her arms. "What are they doing? Why won't they leave me alone?" She ducked her head and stumbled backward. "Make them go away! Oh my Gawd! I've been stung! Get these things off me!"

"What should I do?" demanded Ruby Bee. "Call for an ambulance?"

"Do you have one of those kits?" Estelle said, grabbing Beryl's arm despite the yellow jackets descending like ants at a picnic. "Can you give yourself a shot?"

Beryl fell onto the grass. "Kit's in the refrigerator." Her voice thickened. "Need it now."

Estelle nodded. "I'll get it right away. You just rest easy for a minute."

"I can barely breathe," Beryl gasped. She rolled over and weakly attempted to brush the yellow jackets off her face and arms. "Help me!"

Estelle ran into the kitchen and jerked open the refrigerator door. A carton of milk, a covered dish with leftover pot roast, a bowl of green beans. "Sylvie!" she called as she pawed through bowls. "Where's the kit?"

"Kit?" said Sylvie as she came into the kitchen, rubbing her eyes and yawning.

"Your mother has been stung!"

Sylvie paused. "Oh, dear."

"She says there's a kit in the refrigerator!"

"Then let's have a look, shall we?" Sylvie opened the refrigerator door, pondered the contents, and then closed it. "No, I don't see any kit. Why don't you ask Mother which shelf she put it on?"

Estelle went back to the yard, where she found Ruby Bee twisting her hands. Beryl was still, white, and to be real blunt, as dead as a doornail. "I don't know if this so-called kit might have helped, but I feel like we should have done something," she said as she stared down at Beryl's body. Yellow jackets seemed to be feasting on her as if she were a crumb of cake at a Sunday school picnic. "You'd almost think . . ."

"When they collect the body," Ruby Bee mused, "ain't nobody going to test her skin. She was allergic to bee stings. She went into shock, and she died before she could give herself a shot. Yellow jackets are nasty critters. When riled, they attack. They're a sight smaller than hornets, but they're meaner and more willing to attack."

"Why did they?" asked Sylvie as she sank down on the grass.

"I reckon you know," Ruby Bee said as she folded Beryl's hands over her chest. "You and Buck are gonna have to live with it. I won't say anything. You'll have to decide if a Caribbean cruise is enough to wash away your sins. You have to live with what happened, not me. If the sugar that was meant for the pie ended up in the sunblock lotion, that's not up to me."

"You won't say anything?" said Sylvie.

Ruby Bee gazed at Estelle. "We need to go. If I don't put an apple pie in the oven before long, the truckers will be squawking like jays long about noon. Maybe I'll try an extra pinch of ginger."

"Do that," murmured Sylvia as she went inside the house and closed the door.

Another Room

I come in, tired, frumpy, and disheveled, with my purse, my briefcase, a newspaper, the mail, a sack of groceries, another sack with several bottles of booze, everything all clutched in my arms or in my coat pockets or in my hands, along with my keys. But this is pretty much how I come home every night to my new apartment, and, as far as I can see into the future, the way I always will.

The day has been worse than a nightmare. I am delayed on the subway—not my fault—but this makes me late, and then I can't find the folder with the demographic data before the conference. I know it's on or in my desk, but I can't put my hands on it and my boss gives me this grim look and shakes his head and I feel like a sorority girl who missed curfew. I'm so rattled I spill coffee on my beige suit.

Then my secretary starts in on her personal problems and ends up sobbing in the ladies room most of the morning while I field the telephone. My first client shows up late, which means my second client has to wait, and all this results in a log jam in the reception room—by noon every last person in the office is snickering and I feel like a damned fool. They're lucky I don't have an assault weapon and a lot of ammunition.

But the thing is, I stagger into the apartment, dump my briefcase and the sacks on the sofa, throw my coat on the chair, and automatically hit the play button on the answering machine because I'm supposed to have drinks and dinner with Eddie unless he has to cancel. This is when I see the door.

The problem is that I've never seen this door before. I rented the apartment about a month ago. It's not "condo," but it's all I can afford, this one-room number in the Village. The neighborhood's relatively safe and has a lot of character. The building's old, which means the radiators are balky antiques, but I had to find something after the divorce and opted to pay too much for something trendy so the ex would know I was doing fine on my own.

I blink, but the door doesn't go away. I push everything aside, sink down on the sofa, and rub my forehead. The wall's been there all along, naturally, holding up the ceiling and blocking the view into my neighbors' bedroom. I can hear them, though. They fight, they make up, and then they do a lot of things that make me uncomfortable, but I can't bang on the wall and tell them they're disgusting. There's no law that says you can't behave like mindless animals, that you can't grunt and groan and shriek things that should not be overheard by disinterested parties lying on a Murphy bed all of ten inches away.

But I digress. I'm sitting in the middle of the living room, a bunch of bills in my hand, my machine grinding out messages, and I'm staring at this door. Wood, with top and bottom panels, a doorknob—your basic door. But I'm renting an efficiency apartment in a renovated building and this door is not supposed to be there.

It looks as if it's always been there, right between the bookcase and the television. A really logical location for a door. If there were a separate bedroom, it would be in this precise location. I try to think. I'm fairly certain I'd hung a print there—nothing great, just a Cezanne that I'd picked up years ago. The table with the telephone is now to one side, but it had been centered along the wall as recently as this morning when I rushed out to the subway.

So I'm just sitting, staring at this door. I feel silly, but I look at the baseboards to check for signs of sawdust. I see ten years of dust. My ex used to complain about our baseboards, as if all I did every day was lie on the couch, stuff my face with chocolates, and think of ways to aggravate him when he came home from his hard day at the office. The only thing he forgot was that I'd had a hard day at the office, too. I'm as driven as he, and a damn sight smarter, although that was an issue I tactfully left unexplored.

I'm still staring at this door. Now I think of all sorts of people to call, but I'm having an awkward time with the imagined conversations. It's well past noon, so the super's drunk. My ex is in the Bahamas with his child bride. If I call my mother and say, "Hey, Mom, guess what I found?" she'll be on the next bus from Jersey City, commitment papers in her hot little hand. The more I imagine the announcement that I've just discovered a new room in my apartment, the more I can feel the coarse cotton straitjacket and see the solicitous smiles behind the hypodermics.

I need to think about it. I pour myself a stiff drink of scotch, move the groceries to the kitchen area, empty the ashtrays, gather up the newspapers from last week, stuff dirty laundry in the closet, and sort of wander around keeping an eye on the door.

It's beginning to get dark, and I seem to think Eddie's going to show up soon. I don't remember making the date, but he called yesterday to remind me, which was rather clever of him. He knows I forget things, especially when I'm under all this pressure at the office and not delighted that the ex is remarried and hating to answer the telephone because I'm afraid it's my mother and I simply don't have the energy to deal with her steady stream of criticism. My shrink gave me a relaxation tape and a prescription refill, but I don't really want to relax and I can't take the pills when I'm drinking.

Okay, I tell myself. Open the door and see what's there.

After a minute, I pour myself another drink and sit down directly across from the door. I decide to count to one hundred, then just get up, wall across the room, and open it.

When I get to fifty, I consider waiting until Eddie shows up so we can open the door together. At seventy-five, I consider calling my shrink, but I know from experience I'll get the damn answering service.

Ninety-eight, ninety-nine, one hundred.

My knees aren't at their steadiest, and my hand is shaking as I pour myself another drink, but I go over and make myself try the doorknob. I don't know what I'm expecting—maybe a jolt of electricity or for the door to fly open and a bunch of people from the office to shout, "Surprise!" even though it's not my birthday and we all know I'm not going to see a promotion anytime soon, not after this morning's disastrous conference.

The door isn't locked. I turn the knob very slowly, for some reason feeling it's important not to make a sound, and ease the door open.

The room is dark. I'm not about to set foot inside a dark room that wasn't there nine hours ago. I let go of the knob and feel for a switch.

I find one and flip it up. A light fixture on the ceiling goes on and I'm standing in the doorway of a bedroom. I take one step inside, then stop to study the room. It's small and cozy. There are no windows. There is single bed, neatly made, and beside it a table with a lamp. A dresser, its surface pristine and well polished, and a mirror above it. A wardrobe. An easy chair. An old-fashioned braided rug.

I feel a rush of iciness as it occurs to me that someone might be crouched behind the door. I take a deep breath, let it out slowly, and then look behind the door. All I see is a print on the wall. The Cezanne, oddly enough.

I have to finish the drink before I can go any farther. A little courage—and is it bravado?—sinks in, and I tiptoe to the middle of the room. Although it is exceedingly tidy, there is a sense that it is occupied, although not by a slob like myself. The cushion on the armchair has a slight indentation—someone sits in it, perhaps reading or gazing pensively at the Cezanne.

I'm certain this room doesn't belong to the perverts. There is no other door, not even a closet door, so the only entrance is from my apartment. I get this really bizarre scenario about the previous tenant refusing to leave and vowing to live with me, but without my knowledge. I can almost see her sneaking in and out at night when I'm asleep not ten feet away on my bed, using her front-door key so very cautiously that there's not so much as a tiny click to awaken me.

Yes, the room belongs to a woman. The bedspread isn't ruffly but it has a pleasantly feminine appearance, and now I notice that the chair is upholstered in matching material. On the dresser, there's a vase with an artful arrangement of silk flowers.

I approach the dresser. Unlike mine, there is no dust or scattering of blonde hairs, no jumbled makeup or junk jewelry or bills and work from the office and that sort of accumulation that grows day by day.

I open the top drawer. Here is makeup, but in a compart-mentalized tray. Scarves, each folded into a neat bundle. Several small jewelry store boxes: An unused wallet, still in a box. A few odds and ends of jewelry in yet another compartmentalized box.

She is compulsive about order, I deduce in my best Sherlockian manner. I close that drawer and open the one below it. The sweaters are folded in uniform stacks. I continue to open the drawers and find that each is orderly. Unlike myself, she doesn't have to dig through a drawer every morning to find clean underwear and usable pantyhose. My shrink tells me almost every session that I'll experience less stress if I attempt a degree of organization, both in my apartment and in my mind. I always laugh and assure him that even in the midst of the chaos I know where everything is and that I prefer it that way.

Suddenly I want to burrow through all this neatness, and even pull the drawers out and dump their contents on the floor. Throw the scarves in the air and let them flutter to the floor in a rainbow puddle. Let the makeup clatter on the floor and roll under the chair and dresser. Jump up and down on the bed as if I were a naughty child. Yell profanities to disrupt the ambience of utter serenity.

I quickly close the drawer before I give way to the urge to undo this compulsive woman's handiwork. I am sweating, though, and in the mirror I notice my paleness as I drain the last few drops in the bottom of the glass, wishing for more.

If I leave the room and go to the kitchen to replenish my drink, will the room still be here when I return? If stay here, will she come back and find me in her bedroom? If she does return, she'll be displeased to find an intruder in her tidy, compartmentalized world. Especially an intruder with dirty hair, a coffee splotch on her skirt, sweat stains on her blouse, a run in her pantyhose. An intruder who battles urges with scotch.

I abruptly go out of the room and into the kitchen, where the sight of the bottle helps ease my uneven breathing and my anger. I manage to splash whisky into the glass without spilling it and gulp it down. I put the glass in the sink. Will the room still be there?

Yes, I go to the wardrobe and open its doors. Of course everything hangs neatly and the shoes are aligned in precise rows. The woman dresses well, although with modest discretion. She doesn't stuff dirty clothes in the dark corners and then forget to take them to the laundromat. She is too fine a gentlewoman to wad up sweatshirts and jeans. Her shoes have no mud on them. Her purses, arranged on the shelf, don't have broken zippers and torn straps.

I'm beginning to like her less and less, this trespasser. For that is what she is. It is my apartment, my lease, my extra locks on the door, and my continual fight with the super to fix the leak in the bathroom. Who is she to hide in this orderliness? Why shouldn't she share my frustration when the radiator goes cold and the dripping faucet reverberates and the animals next door begin to groan?

Who she is is what I intend to find out. I slam the wardrobe door and go to the bedside table. Maybe I'll find an envelope with her name, or a perfectly balanced checkbook with her name—and our shared address beneath it. I yank open the drawer with enough anger to make it screech.

There is a Bible. She is pious and self-righteous, I think hotly. She knows I stopped going to church years ago, when I found the confession box claustrophobic and the platitudes nauseating. I can almost see her kneeling in a pew, her gloved hands clasped together, her face aglow with the inner radiance of a madonna.

I snatch up the Bible and open it to the first page to see if her name is written there in perfect script. Nothing. I throw the Bible on the bed and don't give it a second glance as it falls to the floor. She can pick it up and replace it herself.

I feel in the back of the drawer and blink as my hand withdraws, holding a small gun. I have a gun that resembles this one very closely. I bought it when I first moved to the neighborhood. I think it's in the bottom drawer of my dresser, under the sweaters and scarves. Or maybe in the back of a kitchen cabinet.

At least she's worried about being mugged, I think as I examine the gun to determine that it's loaded. Like me, she must lie awake at night listening to the horns blaring and the occasional arguments in the street below, or to the rhythmic squeals of the bed in the next apartment. Like me, she has nights when she can't sleep, when the sheets become damp and the blanket is twisted like a snake around her legs.

I feel better as I imagine her fear. She may not live in a chaos of dirty clothes, unpaid bills, dishes in the sink, dustballs on the floor, and calls from nosy relatives, but she still has a malignancy that swells in the dark and evokes demons.

I decide to steal her gun. Then she'll be even more frightened. After a few nights of insomnia, she'll be clumsy and scatter powder on her dresser. She'll leave clothes on the chair, forget to replace her makeup in the tray, decide it's easier to leave the bed unmade.

I start for the door, smiling to myself. Then I glance at the dresser, and above it I see her. I halt, catch my breath, and move cautiously forward until I'm facing her. Her hair color is much like mine, but she is wearing it in a stylish cut and it shines in the light. She is at least twenty pounds slimmer. Her face is not bloated. Her eyes are clear, with no trace of the redness that greets me every morning.

The worst thing is that she's smiling. It speaks of contempt, and I know that she compares my hair, my face, my body, and my clothes with hers and that she feels superior. She sees the ugly clutter in my room beyond the doorway.

I decide to show her just how messy life can be. I put the barrel of the gun in my mouth. Now I'm going to wait just a minute until I can see that she's beginning to comprehend what I'm about to do. Then I'm going to splatter brains and blood all over the ceiling and walls of her perfect, tidy bedroom.